PRESS DIONYSUS

First published in 2025 by PRESS DIONYSUS LTD in the UK, 167, Portland Road, N15 4SZ, London.

www.pressdionysus.com

Paperback

ISBN: 978-1-913961-47-3

THE WHISPERER

Short Stories

Erinc Buyukasik

DIONYSUS

ISBN- 978-1-913961-47-3

English Translation by Mesut ŞENOL

Press Dionysus LTD, 167, Portland Road, N15 4SZ, London
• e-mail: info@pressdionysus.com
• web: www.pressdionysus.com

ABOUT THE AUTHOR

Born in 1975 in Konya, the writer came into the world as the son of his teacher parents. Following his graduation from the Turkish Language and Literature Department of the Faculty of Letters, Ege University, he started his teaching career in Istanbul. Having begun his writing process with a literary magazine called Düş ve Düşünce (Dream and Thought) he and a group of his friends published, until now the writer's short stories and reviews appeared in publications such as *Varlık, Yeni e, Son Gemi, Ekin San at, Galapera Öykü fanzin, Temrin, Acemi, BroyEski, Edebiyat-ist, Kahverenkli, Yalnızlar Mektebi, Tetkik Dergi, Poesis Edebiyat, Papirus, Yıldız Tozu, Beşinci Sanat, Almanyalılar.net, İz Gazete.* Some of his short stories were included in the following anthologies: "*Kurmacalar Atlası (An Atlas of Fictions)*", "*Lilith Öyküleri (Short Stories of Lilith)*", "*Son Gemi (The Last Boat)*", "*Bir Kaşık Sütlaç (One Spoon of Rice Pudding), Bir Nefes Tarçın (One Breath of Cinnamon).*" The writer published his own short story books entitled as follows: *Söz Dağının Ardındakiler (The Ones Behind the Word Mountains), Suya Gazel (Ode to the Water), Hep Uzak (Always Far Away), Dehlizler ve Rüyalar (Passages and Dreams), Sınırlar Kapalı (Borders are Closed).* His other prose works consist of two novels of *Murat Ka'nın Çoğul Tarihi (Plural History of Murat Ka), Tragedyayı Oynarken (While Playing the Tragedy);* one children novel of *Kuduruk'un Orman Düşleri (Forest Dreams of the Mad);* and a review/essay book of *Kurmacanın Yolculuğu (The Travel of the Fiction).* While keeping on writing regularly in the newspaper called İz Gazete, the writer keeps on his journey of writing as the founder and coordinator of a short story and fiction platform named *+edebiyatkolektifi (+literarycollective).*

His short story book called *Cennet Meselleri (Insanity Parables),* and his book called *Yazının Yol Haritaları (The Road Maps of the Writing)* containing his essays on literature and arts were published in 2024 by Mimas Publishing.

He continuously presents a culture-art program on Haberler. com YouTube channel alongside with Mesut ŞENOL.

For the lost mother smiles in the frames...

CONTENTS

Introduction: A Magician of Short Stories

I had known Erinç Büyükaşık through his short stories, essays and novels. I had also opportunities to get acquainted with him personally during various literary-artistic workshops and gatherings be them in the country or abroad. In particular, his success in research in literature, his ability of composing critical and informative essays with all its peculiarities on a topic or a person in a very short time employing an impressive comprehension, also included in his resource tool kit, had attracted my attention. I would like to add that I was very delighted to see him making good use of his talent by publishing the works of other writers at his literary platforms. I believe the literary criticism and review works have not seen the desired improvement in recent years. Erinç Büyükaşık alone seems to have covered a ground to fill the important void in this field.

The wording of the short stories in this book brings out a unique narration style to the lines, peculiar to Büyükaşık's storytelling – partly difficult to decipher – tasking the reader with some decoding work. This way, a poetical coding is added to the plain turn of expression of the storytelling.

Lastly, Erinç Büyükaşık invites us to join the journey into the inner worlds of the people having varied roles and statuses in social life. In this way, individual and social projections in his short stories transfer fascinating reflections on a common ground to the readers through their personal point of views and biographies.

Istanbul, January 2025

Mesut ŞENOL

Editor

Though Walking is More Difficult

The sounds of the call to prayer are echoing on the stone streets in the silence of the night. The heart of the girl is being shaken by a very thin fear trembling. I can see him again in my dream. Sometimes he fades away like a shadow in the colorless hazy air. As if shadows are crowded inside the house, and his body is being buried into darkness at every step. When looking out of the window, she sees the empty streets in the flickering light of the streetlamps, and the walls of the stone houses leaning back to one another. Nobody is around; the town is asleep without sensing her existence. Whose call to a funeral service is being chanted at this hour? The streets seem to be colder and spooky inside the whispering wind. When she intends to open the window, the deserted house in the town replays in her mind. Burlap sacks flung around, some kind of rusted iron pieces, a long timber drilled at the length of every four finger, leaning against the wall. For sure, they used this room for some time as a closet. She catches sight of three sooty copper pots with their bottoms fallen which were flung around.

She intends to go upstairs by making the wooden stairs creak. Again her nose receives the smell of flour, kind of smell mixed with the thyme, and the fig milk. She hits a sharp light when she opens the window. When looking outside, the sea in the distance seems quite smooth… As if the tiled roofs of the houses are at her feet. After a while, the deserted structure they used to enter for playing in their childhood fades away from her mind.

Whispers, footsteps in the house… The desire of escaping from the town emerges stronger than ever in that night. She is aware that she is after something, but she cannot make it out accurately what it is. By slowly creeping away from the interior of the house, she prepares to go outside. With her eyes full of fear, every shadow appears to her as a threat. The little girl wants to run away, and find herself somewhere outside this town, beyond these dark streets, in a world totally unknown to her.

"Unless I do a thorough cleaning in my memory, my rage turns into the strongest grindstone. It sharpens anything it touches. I get whetted more and more like that girl. I need to hold together these days."

She sends a bit of coldness as she was stepping on the stone ground with her naked feet. As she was toiling to proceed silently in the streets, at every step she gets more fearful, as if shadows are following her, and the streets are getting closed after her. Her heart beats as if it couldn't contain itself, and her hands tremble. Something is stalking, or somebody. Yet when she turns around, nothing is to be seen.

At that very moment, like a shadow, a scary face appearing with a light in his hand. She comes eye to eye with him. As is someone she recognizes. The looks of that man who came out of the town route are cold, and his face seems stiff and decisive.

As she was gravitating towards him, the shadow of the man is getting bigger. By wobbling, the girl would like to take a refuge in a dark corner, then realizing that running away could not go on. As if this darkness which intensifies at every turn coming after her appears to be her destiny. The existence of the man is being felt more and more at every step, as if his breath is being heard at every whisper, at every shadow.

The girl stars to run, but ultimately she gets out of breath; as if the stone streets are holding her tight with their hands, her steps slow down as she goes forward. Recognizing that there is nowhere to run away to, she gets stuck in the middle of the street. She closes her eyes, but that creeping feeling keeps pervading her body. The town watches her silently, and each and every stone wall, every rundown house reflects her fear.

She takes a deep breath for the last time, turning her face with her tear-filled eyes to the sky. The sky seems to look at her mercilessly, like the darkness hanging over her head. At that very moment she realizes that this darkness will always follow and find her regardless of her efforts to run away from it. As the silent scream she is hearing inside her body is blending with the stone streets of the town, she takes a look hopefully at the sky for the last time. As she disappears in the darkness, the town doesn't hear her scream, only the shadows do remember her existence.

The town, silently, buries inside this night full of pain, along-side with other secrets.

I get up with the call to prayer, and I wonder why I was up with the crows. Whereas I was supposed to be idle today. I am still half asleep. All night I saw nightmares. The night before that too… Maybe… By putting my hands on my chest, I listen to that ache coming from the depths of my heart. This sound is such an old, and so much familiar one… Whispers are wandering inside the house, the ones I used to hear, echoing in my memory, not ceasing to stalk me since my childhood. I must have left the curtains open. The dark streets of the town, those old, narrow streets where the houses are expanding like a shadow. I submerge into the void as I look outside. I cock and eye at the end of the street, as if there is a secret, and an untied knot out there.

My hands are callous and covered with coal dusts. At every washing they are abraded more and more, and at every contact with water that deep and cracky sound gets echoed in my mind. I need to do something, such a thing that it could purge me and free me from this heavy load. But how? I don't seem to find the answer yet.

Again, my childhood swarms in the room. My mother used to say, "Childhood is a wound." That old town… The days where everything seemed bigger and scarier. The shadow of my father, that dark facial expression. While combing her hair by the window, my mother outgazes as if she was looking for an escape route out there. When I was a child, I used to watch silently that state of my mother. One night I noticed the frozen fear on her face. She wanted to run away but nevertheless again she couldn't do it. She was like an animal caught in a trap.

Now, I am in the same room with her like the ghosts of the past reside here. I used to believe the existence of ghosts wandering in nights in the narrow streets of the town. The stories of the whispering dead ones through the sound of the wind. There was a little girl once upon a time… That reminds me of the victim children in the witch tales. The dead girls, the secrets of the town… We left her alone as she fell down in that dead-end street while she way running away. From that time on, a silent feeling of guilt has been growing inside me. For sure she is trying to run away, yet while making all those efforts, and hopping up from those huge rocks, her legs are in blood. She extends her hand to me. I look at her whitish face like a stranger. I am coward. A big coward carrying all those secrets. In every nightmare, my fears are growing.

Involuntarily I look in the mirror with its secrets fallen. My eyes… They look at me now like my mother's eyes. My mother used to say, "Childhood is a wound." In that mirror, all the faces of the past appear like a shadow. The silent ghosts lost in the box of the night, and hidden behind the windows. They are nothing but me; me, the child looking out of the window; that girl wanting to be freed, and my mother who cannot run way. All of them are being echoed in me, and behind my eyes.

I am having my prayers sticking in my throat, and the chilliness of water in my hand is disappearing. As if I would always stay by that window, as if I would be petrified with my gaze searching for an impossible way out. The only echoing thing inside the town in the silence of the night is my silent scream as it were.

As the girl was proceeding inside the dark house, the call to prayer reaches into her ears. This sound strangles that unending silence hovering over the town for a moment. The call to prayer seems to guide this little body readying itself to get lost inside darkness by echoing on the streets. The girl speeds up her steps, and her fear increases by each step. There is a shadow coming after her, but when she turns around, only dark and stone walls, the faceless and cold windows of the town look at her.

The sheikh's house built on the top of the hillside leading to the town overlooks the whole town. The sheikh sits on the sofa in his room every morning with the first lights of the day to watch the sleep of the houses. His existence means both a sacred shadow and a silent threat for town folks. Kissing sheikh's hand is a kind of ceremony… Yet it is not allowed to say, "I saw the sheikh", people would only say, "I saw sheikh's hand". Even to come face to face with him is something a beyond reach favor.

While pacing out on the stone streets of the town with fast steps, the girl is sensing that the sheikh's shadow is coming after her. I am at that moment one of the children in short pants running beyond the town until the shore. She was in front of me. *Ready or not, here I come.* She speeds up her steps, as if she is looking for a refuge. As if every street, every stone wall she leaves behind is swallowing her hope. The town is such a location having learnt how to live under the sheikh's shadow, and here it means protection, and a yielding behavior.

She wants to get out of the town, but every dead end street, every corner takes her back to the same place. The streets look like a labyrinth, as if calling her back. The town's folks are asleep, but the sheikh's shadow is being felt behind these streets and stone walls. The people are getting ready to kiss his hand at the time of the call to prayer, whereas the little girl wants to run away and to be freed.

Yet there is no place to run away. Stone streets, dark windows, every corner seem to be filled with the eyes watching her. She couldn't escape from the sheikh's shadow. When she falls down after stumbling on a stone, the creature she thinks stalking her, fully encircles her. Her breathing quickens, her heart throbs. In darkness, on the face of that shadow seems to wear the harsh and cold look of the sheikh. The girl closes her eyes in horror, comprehending that there is no room for her in this world, and she is destined to be forgotten in the silence of the town.

I am looking out of the window. The sky is descending upon us, as if not letting us breathe. I am listening to those old and silent words coming out of the spaewife sitting at the hotel's dim lounge. I feel like I imprisoned myself inside a dream. She holds the coffee cup inside her palms, and I notice tattoos on her fingers. Those strange tattoos her mother crafted when she was small by using quilting needle, milk after childbirth, soot, and gall water… *"Spells of a lost clan"* she says. Each of them hides a secret, every line tells a story.

"Nagehan," whispers the spaewife, "in the village I was born, all women are afraid of losing their children." She repeats the name of the little girl. "They always give birth to fatherless children; their fathers are breaking apart inside the night like an unseen, untouchable darkness. The mothers would not feel the existence of the children clinging to their skirts, by taking a far-off look. After getting up the summits of the mountains, they would descend down the river beds. They are deaf to the voices of the children, and blind to their images. God sometimes makes everyone blind, Nagehan." By pulling on Nagehan's hand, her mother goes forward along the streets. This eccentric girl should be left at her relatives' home for a couple of days. Uncles, sisters-in-law… My daughter used to smell like sweet, says the woman, this time contradicting herself. She had kissed Sheik Sir's hand. Sheikh Sir caressed the girl's cheek by saying "my rose faced, smelling like sweet daughter." Her mother entrusted her to their relatives, is it now possible for the little girl to freely play hide and seek? Every one of them has their eyes on her.

I take a look at the woman's hands. The cub she is holding between her very thin finger seems to get smaller all of a sudden. The pieces are falling down in my mind, and they do not come together. There is a sense of fear I could not make it out. At the very moment I go back to the earlier years; to that town I had spent my childhood, to its narrow street, to its one on the top of the other type of walls, the thin curtains hanging over from its windows. A story behind every window. Nobody is aware of those stories, except those windows are. They stay put silently, elegantly and as much tired as if to say I know those stories. Maybe they did not make their marks in anybody's mind, maybe it is only me always tracking down what is seen by those windows.

The voice of the spaewife is being echoed in my ears. She talks and talks nonstop. How the women of the village lost their children, how their fear turned into a shadow? "Is it you, grandma?" I ask once. She nods her head slowly, and her gaze plunges into faraway places. "Yes" she responds, "she used to tell us like this back in the days. Fears hounding the women, voices coming inside sleep, and unfamiliar faces appearing in front of the eyes… All of them get in our blood."

I take a deep breath. I do remember my mother's hair in the dim light. Chestnut colored, curly and dreamy hair… My grandma used to tell: "Your mother's hair looks like the threads of a dream…" I don't recall it that much. It's only a trace from what I was told, and a shadow surfacing in my mind. But I know, that hair, that smell, all of them are with me. With every step, something inside me gets crashed, and along with every memory, a new wound gets opened. As if I am hung between the options of leaving and staying, and this gripes my soul.

I hear again the voice of the woman. "*You saw a woman who hanged herself*", she says. A repeating shiver inside my body. That woman with chestnut colored curly hair had cut her hair before she hanged herself. The spaewife seems to have known every detail inside that dream. The curly hair cut by the blunt scissors… I turn my eyes away. "No," says my gut. "No, it's not me." But my voice doesn't come out. In fact, I am aware that both this story, these fears belong to me, to my past, to my roots.

I meet with my face in the mirror held by the spaewife. As if in the mirror I can see the woman in the dream. I am scared. My eyes, my hair, every bit of me look like her. The woman realizes it and also seems to enjoy it. My reflection in the mirror, the shadow of the past, all of them is embracing me one by one. I find myself in that dream, in that fear, in that running away. I slowly take my steps. Or else whether everything seems to be so much heavy to me. As if even time forgets to flow.

The spaewife keeps on telling: "*The women of the village,*" she says, "*they all fear of losing the children they gave birth. Having forgotten their own children, they would look after some other people's children.*" These words are like a slap on my face. Even on the occasions of getting lost inside myself, I always search myself in other lives, in other stories. Always something is missing, always half completed.

I close my eyes. Sleeping requires a hard job to do. There is a deep pit inside me. The children getting lost in that pit, the women who cannot face with their fears, a dream looking for itself, all of them are of the rings of the chain. Now I am trying to find my story inside that chain. "Am I also like this?" I wonder. Or else, am I here to be afraid of losing myself? I don't seem to come up with an answer.

I open my eyes with viscous crust. Mine is one of those incomplete sleeps... The spaewife is looking at me, and her eyes are piercing through inside me. Her lips are quivering, with no voice produced. Maybe that voice is already embedded inside me, wandering like an echo in my mind. I am taking a look at my childhood staying like a dream behind the window. "This is my story" I silently tell myself." Yet that spaewife is still in that mirror, as if being lost in those old and timeless stories.

Always Distant

By holding the watch's cordon on his huge belly, Ali took it out from the waistcoat pocket. "It's too late. It's time to head for home," he murmured. A roaring noise rose inside the town's only barroom. Barkeeper Zühtü had turned on the volume of Muslum's album. A few men from the opposite table accompanied the song. With his face turned red, Ali took one more sip. He threw a couple of melon slices into his mouth. His tiny eyes were buried deep into her fleshy face. "To kill or to get killed" he told himself from inside. For a moment, the taste of raki felt like poison. The cigarette burnt her throat. Fortunately, he had come to the barroom alone. Hasan and asshole Recep were not stopping by this place. Had they come, they would have sat facing him, and grinning in a laidback fashion. I couldn't put up with them. They came together two days ago and teased him. Recalling what happened, he sweated out profusely. He felt like drinking water. He had a good mind to drink much more as he kept drinking. The water oozing out from his elongated beard onto his shirt. He started shivering as he broke out into a sweat.

Going away was for sure better than dying here. He would have sent out money to his wife every month, and he would see them a couple of times a year. That would coincide with the holiday periods for sure. While he was in a foreign country, they would obviously take good care of themselves. As his mind yielded to alcohol, his shoulders shrank, and his face turned pale. According to what Hasan said, the factory would be receiving applications for workers at the beginning of the month. His cousin Hüseyin works there, and I swear as a family they don't have any trouble. He didn't share his decision with Emine. There was not an opportunity to open this subject instead of talking about Zehra's incidents every day. What they did would not be considered as a conversation. Wife and husband were bickering.

For a moment, he was appalled by the looks of the persons at the opposite table. As if they are laughing at me in the sleeve. Isn't there any subject to talk about in this big town except my daughter? It's my fault, as I let the cousins step all over me, ours started to envy the boys. Three nights ago, she cried asking, would you love me more, had I been your son. Lately her mother found her in her bed in a state of anger. Having seen blood on her bed sheet, she had mentioned about cutting and killing herself. She began to talk like crazy. Beating her is no good.

He got silent, as if becoming tongue-tied for the last two days. If it is to her mother, the warlock of the village is the only cure. She kept on getting worried that the household necessities became scarce. For sure her mother would be putting ideas into her head. She recently had someone to pour lead to repel evil eye. As if the looks of the girl got lost in void, lifeless lost… She pitied her daughter. Desperation is a pain in the neck. Hasan asked Zehra the other day, "Is yours escaping from the house, I swear it is said that he is going to be a footballer, playing with our boys in other field. Lately he beat Murat badly giving him a black eye. You better have your daughter a boxer or put her on an amateurish team so that there would be some money to help the household. Don't pull my leg Hasan she wanted to tell him that night."

She goggled at him. No way, I have no appetite to deal with these men. By God, I might cause an accident. The man with eyeglasses sitting crosswise might be glaring at me. For a moment, the face of the man looked familiar. Buddy, everyone is just as drunk as a skunk. What do you incubate? Being done in, he was to carry his breath with alcohol to the house. The town's square must me deserted now. If only he would walk down the house. For sure he would feel sober and relaxed.

It's impossible to stay here. There is no money to spend. Leaning to his belly with his hands, he slouched down. As he was trying to get up, a pang, a pain sprung up. You would be a mechanic in a foreign land. The ones at home would not go hungry. The girl went crazy, but do you think his wife is smart woman. She became obsessed with the exorcist, the warlock. Had she gone down the olive grove area and watch the trees streaming towards the sky. With the sparkling stars, she would have dreamt of them until the light beams would be going down the hill towards morning.

Many dreams she already had forgotten would pass through her mind. You cannot shape life the way you wish. The girl has been defying the boys of the town, and he cheered up for a moment since she is not a feeble person. The town folks are poking fun at the situation. Masculine Zehra here, Masculine Zehra there… He always prayed God to have a son when Emine was pregnant. Did the God Merciful mistake his wish. Far from it, he said to himself when his mind became fuzzy. Heavenly only knows why. Even though God created a defective one, this should be considered a test for us. Emine had already started preparing the girl's bundle. Her bundle ought to be ready, Zehra had said. If the daughter would not marry a right guy, then she would end up with a disorderly man, and from him many naked children like a pup. He put out the cigarette by pressing it on the full ashtray under his nose.

Her nose was not that ill-shaped and very flat. She just didn't like his face in the mirror. She keeps fighting with small children. I swear she became like fighting roosters. Moreover, she started smoking cigarette with the boys. A spark appeared in her mother's eyes. We got ourselves talked about by the town folks. Again, he said prayer when he was prostrating. She started visiting the cemetery with niece Murat. They took Mehmet, the bastard of corn chandler along. Town's women in robe can keep talking and talking. The daughter of the pander, you filled the household with the jinnee. No-never! You cannot interfere with God's business yet are all the relaxation and abundance just for other households? Why on earth does welfare not stop by their two-room house? Last evening, the rat brought by the striped cat in its mouth was parading in her hand, hovering around the garden. Throw it away girl, I said but in vain. I did make her throw that pest after beating her. She would sometimes talk to the roosters and hens in the poultry house. That hair of her in the closet. How come she sacrificed her hair by cutting. She had found the girl in the room bare-naked. When she clobbered her and exclaiming, die, go to hell, yet the girl did not say a word. How did you do this bloody girl!

She kept repeating her curses. She was counting her beads on one hand and praying for patience on the other hand. "Subhanallahi ve bilhamdihi, sübhanallahi'l azim..." Like a broken record, she repeatedly said the prayer. First Fatiha then Ayete'l-Kürsi... I submitted to you all of my needs, I glorify you by saying your name is Rasul-i Ekrem... You are gracious... The gardener asked Saint Enes, did you see anything in the sky? It was covered with the cloud and rain... Saint Enes had the gardener get on the horse and touring around, the rain had not reach beyond the Gadban Palace. This is just the will of God... May God bless you with wisdom. As being pushed away from the closet, the lunatic was just laughing. Recently, mom, the blood came, she lamented. Obviously, she doesn't seem to be a fan of studying. This girl is going to get us into so much trouble as she grows older. She insists on not wearing a skirt, would it be alright to go to school in shalwar? I wasn't able to convince my man. Even I wanted her to go to the mosque to be more knowledgeable about godliness, science and become a hafiz, but in vain.

At that night, the eyes of the girl were glassy. Like a dead. By hardly wrapping her with the bristle blanket, she took her out of there. She was shivering by covering her bald head with her hands. She had a high temperature. When her head was raised from the prostration position, the woman thought of what sin we committed my God, why did you put us in trouble. As she was putting the prayer rug away, she noticed that the girl was in the other room. Rolled into a ball, she was lying in the bed. By squatting on the sofa bed, four thousand times *selaten tefriciye*… Why on earth this girl is lying on the bed like a dead person? They didn't give us peace of mind. This time I need to say the prayer four thousand four hundred forty-four times. While all of these were passing through her mind, Zehra talked in her sleep in the bed. Her voice was giving away her sickness. The crazy girl was seeing so many things in her dreams, who knows? Her eye caught the glimpse of geraniums in the garden. The cat leapt on the wall, and jumped on the roof. Look at this ignoble animal, it would scare one at this hour.

My grandma grumbled using a murmuring voice, sit ting with her stick on her chin on the stone-floor. Weeds and snapdragons are grown in the cracks. My grandma looked at me with pity and cursing. Crazy is here. Recently I dug the soil of my grave. I dug is deep in a rage and resent fully. Mehmet made fun of me. I took out big stones, and my fingers bled. Blood drops were fallen on the ground. My hair is short. "You look like ugly boys" my mother said as she was beating me.

"Are your breasts are getting bigger" smirking, my cousin looked at me, too close to me. He wanted to touch that place. His hand wandered inside of his underpants. "Would you like to see mine?" he just asked. Go away, pander, I snapped. Buddy, act decently, I started to get on him and I clobbered the boy.

He cried in front of me. It hurt me so bad in my heart. I washed my muddy and blood-stained hands with the water streaming in full flood just a bit further the mulberry tree. "Take put your thing into one of your places" I had told him while I was punching his face. A rooster is walking in the garden. My mother is always distant to me, at this house, the men always call the shots. Had they had a son, my father would have had him carried on his head and back. While my mother was craving during pregnancy, my father kept wishing to have a boy. I, on the other hand kept waiting in distant corners to catch my father's smiling looks. How come a girl would beat the boys out. She stood under a deep purple star cloud as she was thinking about all of these.

Recently my mother and the neighbors went to the mosque for religious interchange ceremony. They are to save me from this evil. My mother doesn't speak to me. She keeps scolding me saying it would be the one to go crazy, but you did not let it be that way. You were born in difficulty, I cursed a lot when you were coming out of me, it was obvious then that you would be a trouble to us.

As the door of the room the light falls inside. My mother is walking about in the other room by pulling her scarf at both ends. She coiled up on the bed. Something kept wiggling inside of her. You need to be strong, with this child state, you need to be astute. My father doesn't like crybabies and the halfhearted. My mother is again murmuring the prayers, continuously walking in the room holding the Koran in her hand. May God forgive, the ignoble ones. They had a verbal assault on that small girl. In a few years' time she is going to become a big woman, still she is head-in-the-clouds. With her shoulders collapsed and exhausted, she watched the fussy steps of her mother in the other room. Her mother was walking with wobbling steps as if she was in a vacuum.

She was riding off in all directions in the room. On the pale face of Zehra, an untimely sweat landed. Mother, blood came out, I don't like to grow I swear, the woman hood is not developing inside me, it doesn't find its place in me. You are going to get me married in a couple of years. I myself did cut them, when prolonged I feel nauseated. Should I have enough power, I would have cut my breasts too. I just stood inside the cupboard just like that naked. My body is fighting with my soul.

Three hens and one rooster, in all. Her mother had asked her not to forget to give their food. Let them wander in the garden. Three to five eggs for one sack of wheat. You would live on if you can breed, this is the law of life. It hurt so bad in her heart when she thought about this. She doesn't have the inclination to marry although her el der sister had the opposite thought about it. At her age of fifteen, she got married as soon as she graduated from the junior high school. She had told that you cannot stay at this house anymore, Halil, a distant relative, is a good guy, she had to say. What is this liking for playing the ball, girl? Stay at home after school. Help your mother with the household chores. Those boys though, were not as good as her at playing the ball. Look at those boys trying to show off. Apparently, they don't want me among themselves. They keep complaining about me to their fathers. The manhood is not harbored only in the body. If only the hens would stop laying eggs, then they would be in trouble. Do not let them marry me, and let those dirty, ugly boys be near me. Those hens got used to eat from my hand. They listen to me in the coop as is I share with them a secret. They stop chucking as soon as I begin to talk. For a few days the rooster discontinued his crowing. I don't know whether he pitied me or not.

When he was out of the barroom, the patchy clouds had surrounded the sky. There is a road stretching along the several shrubs, olive groves on the way home. In the shady places, a couple of dogs are asleep with their bodies spread. Hey guys, the devil is in our minds. As it were, the girl has been pestering the boys of the neighborhood. You bastards, you sons came near the girl by wagging their tails. Yes, Zehra had been a bit ill-tempered for some time, for sure this town drives her crazy. What was it for that she paraded that rat in her hand? It's not good to beat her, neither is good not to beat her. In the end, she will suffer and die if I beat her badly. He took out his cigarette. When he smoked, the first breath felt bad to him. This damn thing is not that innocent. He should not have smoked this much. He gazed off into the vies of haw trees, poplar trees, and olive groves around him. Not being able to stand, he collapsed on a stone. He tidied the lower parts of his shalwar. He put his feet into the creek streaming meagerly. He pulled himself together at that moment. He slapped his face with water. There is a gate of this village, and you enter from here, yet finding the other gate is impossible. The cemetery on the heel turns out to be the other gate most of the time.

Recently, they had seen the girl walking around the shrubs near the cemetery, in his father's bolero and a big salwar. The girl started smoking the cigarette. She should have been a boy, being more manly than the boys of the village, she would be telling everyone like this. She walked up to all of them saying have you become a true man with your dick. She made the cat with wet nose at home, and the poultry in the coop her company. She wanders in the streets with his bald head. The fourth glass didn't good to him. We should go, if I can put things in order, then I could take the girl and her mother along my side. I have no intention to die here. Let us get away from here. For a moment, he calmed down under the stars and multicolored clouds of the sky. Cannot you see the blunders the crazy girl, what an ignoble man you are. He remembered that his wife is always grumbling over his head. Should I kill the poor woman? Look, she is just all skin and bones. Do not take it seriously that she would beat those boys. He collapsed on the old rag left by the children. At the lower part of his eyelashes and at the tips of his eyes, some white crust had been accumulated. The tears started streaming from his eyes. He was crying for the first time. That big man wanted to cry as much as he would like. He took a look at the sparkling stars.

After taking the quilt and the bed out of cupboard she carried them with difficulty to the roof, and let her body fall on the bed. Quite a warm weather. She took refuge in the warmth of the bed. Were her father's hands hot? Yes, they were callous. When his hand hit her face, the force of the hand felt hard and merciless. She remembered that she never slept on the bosom of her mother. His father entered the garden, the gate of the garden was kicked. The cat meowed in a rage. He is drunk again, soused. The songs, tunes. She was scared at that moment. I hope he would not mess with me. She overheard that his father was grumbling and cursing his God and his fate. I really promise, I would become a true daughter, marry me to a man like my elder sister. I will not embarrass you in front of everyone, I swear… She folded down inside the bed. She covered her face with her hands. He is one of those father smelling tobacco. Always distant… Her bluish eyes shrank as these thoughts were crossing in her mind. Her mother kept saying her prayers in the bed on the floor. The guy shouldn't drink alcohol anymore; he should vow not to drink it again. Let him go to hell, she thought. Then she closed her eyes. Trying to sleep, she stirred around in the bed.

He stopped at the head of the bed on the roof. He rubbed his eyes with his two fists. His daughter inside the bed is folded down. When asleep, her father would not touch her. Her throat got dry out of crying. She put her head on the pillow as light as a feather. He wanted to embrace her daughter. He was frightened by his decision. It was enough for him to watch her in the dark. The wind blew at that moment. The trees, the olive groves fluctuated as it were. A rustle has spread around.

Are really the stars multiplying? One shooting star presently followed by another one.

Buried in the bed, Zehra made a wish at that moment. His father too, as he was waiting inside the dark...

I am so Good

The dolmush moved on along the asphalt route by murmuring and rocking as though on a spring. A pile of vehicles, busses with their passengers inside are in wait at the non-advancing traffic in the grayness of the city stretching out of the dolmush's window. So many roofs, chimneys, windows passed by as they proceeded bumper to bumper. I am being tempted to turning off the engine and get out of the vehicle. Let the ones inside the dolmush do what the hell they are doing. The same torture every day at this hour. The ones inside the dolmush are exhausted, waiting uneasy with their half completed sleep. The rain doesn't seem to stop. There is not an available space to stand up since the Dolmush collects passengers at every step. Everyone was waiting silent and cowering body to body, side-to-side in this stalled traffic. Shrunk on her seat, Zeynep was angry at herself. How on earth did she miss the shuttle vehicle? Was this the best place for her to have sat behind the driver's seat. Now the ones sitting in the back seats would be sending the dolmush fare through me. She is still half awake. The day started somewhat troublesome. When the alarm went off, she wanted to sleep a bit more, and she kept turning around in the bed. Five more minutes, five more minutes. It was most likely that she would be late for work. The boy on her left side, appearing thirteen or fourteen years old, had yielded himself to sleep with his eyes closed while seated and his face towards the window. For sure, he was just out of his work or he was up all night and now heading for work. Without moving, he was opening his eyes from time to time, and then he was plunging into sleeping. She would always have envied such adept sleepers.

Leaning his left elbow against the open window, Burak was smoking at that very moment. With a distressed face he waited for the green light. Would it matter if the green is on now, no doubt, he would be caught by another red light. His eyes searched for an alternative road to get away via highway. He looked daggers at the passenger to get off at Ümraniye intersection. We are stuck now in this vehicle swamp at this hour because of this guy. Let this asshole walk one or more steps, he said to himself silently. Dude, why don't you check these tires, ha! They became bald again. I told daddy, dude. There is a problem in the gearbox. Can you hear the sound? While searching stations on the radio beneath Burak, Ramo gave ear to the sound. He nodded. At that moment he watched Burak with an uninured look. Look at that guy, he sits in this cold weather wearing a very thin shirt wide open. For a moment, he was annoyed by this state of his friend. In earnest, the gearbox is singing bro. Even daddy heard the sound, if you will. He evaded by saying we can take it to the mechanic shop.

Zeynep came eye to eye with Burak. He is very handsome kid, I swear! She might seem to know him somehow for sure. The raindrops were splashing on the roof of the vehicle. A heavy and touching music piece from the radio got around. Burak scolded Ramo by saying "Don't play with this radio, buddy! Oh, cistak cistak, you have no sense of measurement dude." Suddenly a fainted sweat odor filled the dolmush. One more time, many guys whose bodies have not seen water filled the vehicle in this morning. Zeynep wrapped her scarf around her nose tightly, and made an effort to pull at both ends of her skirt which in no way could not reach her knee. She tried to cover her uncovered legs with her coat. The cold wind coming out of open window slapped her face for a moment. The amulet attached to the rear view mirror swung while dolmush was moving.

Burak waved the rosary he was holding in his left hand a couple of times. The road seemed to get opened. When a red jeep suddenly overtook dolmush and plunge into the middle lane, the vehicle was flung on the road for a second. He cursed out at that moment. Hey buddy, the bastard is going to make us make an accident in the morning. "Pal, can you see this bastard driving this jeep! If only that vehicle would have been mine. Daddy gets on my nerves, and he would not let us have some share from the revenue. As if I am one of the high school baby. He started giving me just the pocket money. Since I can spare some of the daily earning so that I can afford buying cigarettes." He was going mad when one of the newly getting on dolmush extended 50 lira banknote. He snapped at the man saying, don't you have change bro?

Grumblingly he put down the banknote, and then after organizing the money compartment filled with note and change money, he arranged the change. At that in stance he swiftly extended the change to Zeynep without looking at her face. Zeynep handed down the change to the passenger behind her. Yes, this was how she remembered that boy!

They were exchanging messages on the chatroom of the internet. Really, he told her that evening that he was working at his father's dolmush. She did not know him anyway. He was really a wiry boy, being as handsome as the ones in photos. She was rarely getting on dolmush. See that coincidence. While you are going to the work by the shuttle, and one day you are forced to get on dolmush. And this man shows up being its driver. In the chatroom she had posted her photo with a hazy and unclear face. No, he did not recognize her at all. Yesterday he had insisted to her that she would be posting another photo of hers. For some days he has been sending some poetry pieces to her. "Yesterday I gave all the earning to daddy. He just gave me 20 Liras. My son, I save money for your wedding, or else I know you are big spender." Ramo looked at him grinningly after these words. He would know when they finished the bottle. There were times that Burak would foot the entire bill to put a bold face on it. "I swear Ayşe came it with you seriously. The veteran Casanova is going to tie the knot." "Dude, don't ridicule me. Leave it there, shall we go to our barroom again this evening?" Zeynep was unavoidingly overhearing the talk between Burak and Ramo. She tried to hide her face with the scarf. He is engaged so to speak. He was writing to the girl for weeks. Poems, big words... He even mentioned that he was looking for a friend for life.

They were going to meet in Kadıköy tomorrow. Let me shit on my mind, he said to himself silently. Burak swore again when the commercial vehicle overtook his dolmush. He honked the horn at length. "Hey, I would take out Haydar in the end because of these commercial vehicles. How that crazy punk took over without putting on the signal?" All passengers startled with a deafening noise.

As he attempted to brake so suddenly, the vehicle was flung. Zeynep felt that her inner body had almost come outside. An oldest man wearing a cap, sitting just behind the girl, snapped at Burak "Hey son, use the damn break slowly!" Silently grumbled that as if he was in a hurry to take shit to the tannery. Murmuring a prayer to scold the boy, he said: You should not give them a driver's license. Other passengers, in utter silence, looked at the old man like the sheep to be sacrificed.

Müslüm was singing his song on the radio station by crying. Zeynep had plunged into thoughts again. This month they were supposed to deposit the Premium. His father was going to pay the bank instalment for the mortgage. My daughter, you either get married at this age or else you are going to get old I swear. She had difficulty to understand why her mother had a huge desire to get her married. She had found a job as soon as she finished her school. Was she a burden in the household now? Burak changed the frequency of the radio ragingly. He was in forming another driver friend of his about the key roads in traffic via the telephone he had leant against his ear. Maltepe intersection is not moving bro, we waited for half an hour, believe me. The song called "Men Don't Cry" started playing on the radio. I love the voice of this woman for as long as I've known. "Dude, you made me feel un easy with this kind of music." If there is someone to get off at the traffic lights, let him get off here. Göztepe intersection costs two seventy-five my sister." Say that the guy was going to get married. The rain drops were hitting the window angrily, the weather got crazy again. "Daddy submerged in the past recently, and he did not surface yet. In good old days, we would commute between Şişli and Pangaltı driving those Desotos. Without feeling shame, you are turning up your nose at Ford Transit. He got that plate number for me, ha… Saying this is bread and butter son, he is rubbing my nose in the dirt, you see." Ramo nodded for what Burak had to say. He was listening admiringly to all of his talk from the very beginning of the road. Ramo was sallow one with a shrunk shoulder. In every sticky response to Burak, he would become more hunchbacked in Zeynep's eyes. "Dude, he would not be unjustified." Burak made a grimace as opposed his friend's reply. "Anyway, leave it there, really who is that girl you are chatting? You are such a phenomenon I swear." Burak smirkingly smiled at him. He had the luck of the devil, again he made up with him. As he was tightly holding the steering

Wheel with his both hands, the road was already cleared, and the traffic had started to flow.

For a moment his hand wandered on the gear shift. His eye perched on the writing of "Bismillahirrahmanirrahim" hung on the rear-view-mirror. His father had put it there four years ago. His turquoise eyes appeared in the mirror. No way, she could not have recognized me. On that photograph, his hair was in chicken yellow color. "She is a stone cold fox bro. I didn't see her face, but her buttocks, her breasts are wonderful. Dude, we are going to meet with your brother's wife tomorrow. Look, I recorded her photo in my telephone." Taking a look at the photo, Ramo's eyes popped out of his head. "This woman is somebody bro. Truly this girl is beautiful." "You licked your lips, as I can see. Hey give me back that telephone." Even though she was tensed for the talk about herself, Zeynep liked the fact that she was deemed beautiful. Burak was seriously giving all of his attention to the traffic at that moment. He blew a horn at the commercial vehicle trying to overtake his dolmush. "Dude, everything is permissible in our masculinity lexicon. I didn't tell the girl that I dropped out of the high school, just for your information. Maybe one day you may run into her, do not ever give it away. The woman thinks that I am a student of the open university." Then he started to wave rosary once or twice he was moving inside his palm. As two passengers were getting off at the stopping point, a fresh air entered the interior. The rain had started to thicken in earnest.

How did this guy deceive me for a week? As if he would open up his accounting office as soon as he would graduate. Arrange a bachelor's pad for me these days. Who knows, maybe I need to take your brother's wife for coffee drinking." The yellow centipede burst into laughter when he heard what Burak had to say. Zeynep felt that she blushed to the roots of her hair. She was trying to watch the streaming traffic out of the window. No way, she was being late for work. I should have not heard; after all he did not recognize me. She angrily squeezed her both hands. She was nibbling her lips feeling as mad as hell. There is not much left. I would be getting off in five or ten minutes. "Dude, if your father would not have caught you red-handed with the girl, then there was no way for you to get engaged." Burak's face assumed a serious look, his face shrank. "Anyway, we are going to suffer the con sequence." At that moment Burak swore at the motorbike rider overtaking his dolmush by speeding. He put the gear into forward speed. The dolmush accelerated as if it was entering a rally.

"What do you make of the goal Fener received? While playing away." It was because of the bastard referee, dude. It wasn't a fault, for one thing. You would eat someone's dust for sure, if you put Sen Jayson as the builder of the middle field. There is no player's fabric in that guy." When they detoured from the main road to the side street with the stretch of four-five story apartment buildings, the tires entered the hole turned into a mud swamp. "When your father went to the pilgrimage, he furnished the dolmush with all sorts of prayers." "His head is always in prostrating position. Bro, let me have you get off over there at the lights. If there is nobody getting off at Haydarpasha, I would be using short-cut way. Nobody in the dolmush said anything. Zeynep was angry with herself deep down inside. My mother asserted it rightly that one needs to judge a man not according to his stature but his standing. Look at this sinister man's malignant looks. As if he was going to eat me... She closed her eyes at that very moment. If only the fight inside her would have stopped. A big pain was stabbed her head. She wanted to forget those two eyes in the rear-view mirror. As the dolmush was jolting, she felt that she was diminished as opposed to the huge buildings outside. How is that yellow centipede faced man was grinning wolfishly as his friend was talking? He is the third wheel of that guy. Stretching himself, Burak tried to relax. "My whole body got stiff. In the end, I will be stranded with this bucket of bolts." As she was getting off hurriedly through the middle door, the exhaust smoke left by the suddenly moving dolmush, went down the wrong way. While getting off, her eye caught the writing on the window. "Sometimes it's necessary to start from all over again." You are such a fan of wise sayings, you bastard. Aren't you a man, you all need to be destroyed. The clouds over Haydarpasha were nesting together like dirty cot ton bales. When she headed for the hilly road, she realized that she was walking with her shoulder lowered. For a moment she felt like crying. She was frightened of her state. She straightened her back. She looked at her watch. Fortunately, she was not late for the office. The rain also had subsided. I am fine, fine indeed.

The Ones I Wove in the Multicolor of the Evening

Though I don't like any rulership
Under the power of the stove
Clashingly in any case
The girls who can blossom
Well-behaved, calm, waiting to die
Gülten Akın

I did knit this net in this apartment. A crammed house. All of my memories clung to my nets is my graveyard. I tied every knot trying hard and minutely. She was grumbling when she was alone. She was resenting her regrets You are welcome to the semi-open prison. She could not leave the house even she wanted. Even though several times she held the girl from her arm, asking her to take her to the market, yet her niece paid no heed to that request. She didn't have no strength left to go down three stories alone. Plop plop plop. This monotonous sound was tiring. You see the spring rains started again. It would continue persistently for days. The water leaking from the pipes created already a small puddle on the window sash. Two doves would come by next morning. I feel cold again. Combi boiler are burning like crazy. With this thought she put on her loosely knitted wool cardigan. Ah her rheumatism illness, she murmured. The girl had come in the morning and prepared the dish, and then after having chatted with her for one or two hours, she had left the house. These pains are the confirmation of being old. Keriman Bey, that man appearing easygoing, would not mention about your being hyppish, and being a bit vixen. The cats are meowing hysterically. Dirty animals waiting for their females underneath the soffits. Aren't you male, you all are the same. I am celebrating thirty-fifth anniversary of my loneliness, accumulating and growing after the guy who years ago left the house. Cling cling, cheers… Yet, after all, I am one of the women who could stand on my own legs alone. If I want to kill myself, it would be my decision. The guy has got now his family, grandchildren, yet my quarrels with him still revisit my mind. His state looked pathetic, and he is panting. His coughing got stronger again. The rain hits the window madly. She took out her thin cigarette she couldn't give up out of the silver case, at the instance she can't help looking at the view of the pouring rain

The pain on her neck seems to go down to her chest. What's worse, slowly and slowly. What if it could take her to another world? No, the slowly spreading pang bodes no good. She examined that part of her body with her right hand. Maybe there is only time for couple of breathing left. Anyway, she sits in her single seat. Dying there gave her a sense of peace. At her refuge, at the corner she chose, she thought, one should kick the bucket. Your husband did not leave you below the breadline. The rest is stuff and non-sense. Her late mother was one of the women who was addicted to the guys who consider her daughter deserving to chiffon sheets, silk nighties. It was not in vain that she closed her eyes to their marriage in those years. The poor woman had no experience of having a duvet, chiffon sheet in her life. After all, her father was a government employee who was mean enough to steal a penny off a dead man's eye. She caught sight of the lacework at the corners of the antimacassars, she had made them all by herself. How many years passed: She couldn't remember it for a moment. What is not she could remember lately? Şerife, her only visiting neighbor, had told her that these are the work of handicraft. At the moment when the pain in her chest had gone, she too liked the designs on the laced tips. She would do just in needle work. Two straight, one reverse… She had learnt that needlework from her late mother. Pains. Lately they became unending. All of here organs seemed to have lost their resistance so to speak. She has been suffering from rheumatism for four years. She tried to rub her calcified legs. She likened herself to an ugly, skin on top of skin type of freak, weak trinket. The tall dressing mirror in the hall would not lie to her, right. Ah Keriman Bey, chatty, word master. The monument of slowcoach in the bed, as if all the sins and crimes belong to me. I didn't appreciate you enough. Why didn't you forget about the time forty years earlier? Those were the shitty years. For sure he would be about to die. His only wife would always be making the sublingual medicine. He has two daughters. Years ago he made both of them married. He just plunged into the job of fatherhood when he saved himself from me. Her reflection in the mirror cursed him while all of these were crossing her mind. At that moment she tried to reach the water glass on the coffee table. If only one or two sips she would take. For some days, she feels that she is losing her strength. It's in vain even Şerif would say, you would send us to graveyard. It's time to move she thought. She heard that under the dim light of the street the heartbreaking screams of the cats invaded all the place. If still he would be hearing those noise, then there is hope. As she buried herself in the seat, she deemed the cats as the indication of life.

During mid-day, she insisted to her niece to doll her up. The poor girl, applied under-eye concealer on the woman's shrunk under eye area, and she administered small touches upon her insistence. She had told her to hint mischievously that she is still of some beauty. She did not forget to get her to put a light colored powder on her face. Eventually if you are to die, then one should go to the other side beautiful and well-groomed. She remembered the time a couple of months ago, when she did her makeup by guess and by golly without looking in the mirror. A couple of months earlier, with pulp powder, mascara, pens and lipsticks she had tried to look younger. Ah the plump lips of my youth, Belgin Doruk's eyebrows, rouge on my cheeks, misty looks. Everything seemed to have died alongside with that cursed guy's leaving the house.

The sparkling glance of the years of youth from end to end on the wall. The photographs are nailed askew. Every photo reflects the loose happiness. All of those memories now amounting to nothing but a pile of nausea, and crying inside. Each of those photos are already gathered dust. This girl would have dusted them from time to time to have their younger state appearing. She would consider her years in those times with pride. That slick-chick woman with mini skirt had always suffered from the men. She thought about that she was as unfortunate as her late husband. She also thought about her poor mother, who was oppressed under her father's empire, a woman just all skin and bones. So many bad traits were transfers to the daughters from their mother. This is such a misfortune. She was not luck in her youth as far as the guys are concerned. In the end, she got the notoriety of being a frigid woman in the neighborhood. After divorcing her husband in one sitting, she didn't feel like sleeping with another man. Oh such a stupidity. Shit, why did you stick to Keriman Bey in this way.

Her shoulders with thin bones shivered. Though the window was tightly closed. She tried to take a deep breath. Why are you clinging to this life? She thought about the fact that as long as you can swallow, then there is something worthy of living. She should get rid of those big sad ness, old brokenness, and enough is enough expressions from this house. Tomorrow let me warn the girl to clean the house properly. Every nook and cranny of the house. The people in the building consider her for some time as a stocker. The interior of the house looks like a memory graveyard. The memories can't be so easily discarded. They say many things about her, she had her niece tell her everything to her under coercion last evening. Şerife happens to be such a gossiper, being a talebearer. Silent, discreet, stocker. Her husband used to curse about her being silent though.

- Don't you have your tongue honey? Don't you ever speak?

The affectionate words of the honeymoon period would be replaced in time with anger. The guy didn't have any resemblance to that handsome actors kissing Belgin Doruk. She recalled the times when she closed her eyes not to see his fatty and slouching body during their marriage. She would tell herself, let him go through, and endure it. Furthermore, she was happy his being one of the husbands coming home late every day. From those nights on, her taking the men, she had never seen their faces before, into her bed started in her dreams. Had he not made innuendos when coming home, then she would have put up with Keriman Bey... She remembered that all the nice and soft words were reserved for the men in her dreams during those years. She cheered up at that moment by recognizing her making Kerim Bey suffer a lot.

- When did you smile at your husband, ha? When did you say to him, my beloved husband? You were like a fridge in the bed. Moreover, you were not fertile.

In fact, she wanted to laugh all the time. As her father was telling them that the girls would not laugh for all to see, causing her to tend to forget to utter words. It is such a huge burden for a human talking to his or her in side. When she was a girl like an apricot branch, she used to sing silently in high volume. During happy seasons of those years she had laughed as much as she wanted. Violets, roses, geraniums in vases got withered once she got married. As those years paraded in her mind, she hardly sipped the water on the coffee table, she is not to delay the timing of the medication. She tried to melt the blue and red ones inside her mouth. The sour taste made her feel sick at her stomach. The girl was supposed to come in the morning. She had told her not to stop by in the evening. Her niece would pay heed to her, in her crazy times. After saying that again her aunt's time arrived to seclude herself, she put a big kiss on her aunt's cheek and left the house. On the radio, the song called, "Farewell Kiss" was playing. She hummed a bit. While humming, her voice went out off the tone.

"Well, while you are about to leave me, you should not have shown that orphan face."

She took a look at the cloudy, sprinkling sky in the multicolored evening. Again, the darkness and the rain reflected from the only window of the house catching the sun distressed her. The March cats were driving the neighborhood with their naughtiness. She envied the cats. After a while one would envy those disgusting animals by being jealous of them. Every one of them are attending their business in front of the public. Nobody says anything. The sense of tingling in her body doesn't bode well. At that very moment she sank on the chair. Her pains got out of hand. She found herself inside a sweet dream. She dreamt of her skinny but feminine body in the strong arms of Murat, a man in his fifties, the son of Saniha. This crazy dream started visiting her very frequently on recent days. At first, she was surprised to see her more feminine state as opposed to skinny and saggy woman in the mirror. Still attractive and beautiful considering her age. That is to say that despite many years passed yet she was able to remain more feminine compared to those darling, affectionate old ladies. Murat was kissing her on the lips lewdly. As the guy was roaming between her legs using his hands, the woman's groaning was amplified. As she was feeling the man hood of Murat who was grasping her breasts and tights with his big hairy hands, she was happy to realize that the desire inside her body did not fade away during those passing years. When Murat paid a visit for several times alongside with Saniha, he had smiled tongue in cheek, I swear. He wasn't born yesterday. Even though he kept saying "aunt", he was hiding different things in his looks. Something looking for and desirous. For some time, the more she was thinking of those looks, the more she was feeling out of ordinary. Now they are in the same bed, naked, in the strong arms of the man. When the raw yellow color of the street lamp hit the bed, they were panting. Ah these dalliances, love games. They seem to make humans to hold on to better the life. Their breathing got faster. As she was landing wet kisses on the man's bearded face, a sharp pang descended down her heart. The nakedness of the man in her dream wandered in her mind for the last time.

The locksmith had worked hard to open the door. Sister Şerif, these locks are very old, let me try to open through this wire. Growlingly he forced to the lock. He thought about it as if it is the gate of the prison. When the door was finally opened through the wires in different lengths, a huge creaking sound was heard. The smell of death turned the swarming neighbors' stomach. All of them threw a look at the rigid face as white as a sheet out of pity. Apparently, her niece did not stop by yesterday. No, the girl, the poor girl already called me. Even though she knocked at the door so many times, the deceased must have not opened the door. Probably the key of the girl was lost.

- Hey neighbor, there is such a weird smile on the face of the diseased.

With the Indistinction of the Mind

She realized that what she remembered became indistinct when her eyes caught sight of the third and fourth stories of the shanty housed surrounding the street through the window. The sun is about to set. Kemal would come back from work in a couple of hours. He would ask if the dinner is ready while he was taking off his shoes by the door sill. Let him eat shit. Really, which one goes well, tomato or pepper paste in cooking. She was lost in thought for a moment holding her hands on her knees. She startled by Nesrin's voice. Ours dozes off most of the time by spreading his buttocks. Anyway he desires me once in a while. Moreover, he would close and lock all the doors to make sure that children cannot hear what would be going on. She started laughing as she was sloping up her tea. For days, you have stayed at home like a tower owl.

Ask Kemal to take you to the park or a place by the sea. Prink up yourself a bit, put on your best bib and tucker. At least go for a walk, and take the air. Hey girl, like this, staying at home would drive you crazy. Is it something that my thick-skinned man would do something about it? May the guy kick the bucket. Her thoughts became fuzzy, and a huge feeling of loneliness accumulated inside her. The odd liveliness and enthusiasm in Nesrin eyes got lost in an instance. She too went off the boil. The joy of a moment ago died down when she noticed Nesrin's silent state. Suddenly, absentmindedly her eyes glued to the crowd of women and men who were frightening on television. Your cake tastes great neighbor, is it with carrot? Let me have its recipe today. She also entertained herself with what she had to say. She had taken the recipe of that cake from Nermin maybe a couple of times before. Just for the sake of conversation.

How many years ago had she come on board the boat? Was it last year, or the year before. The word year seemed unfamiliar to her. Everything is indistinct in his mind. That day they were on the island boat. Even around noon, the sun was over their head. First she had thought that the big houses lined up along the Bostancı shore were lost by getting melted from the dazzling light of the sun. She had closed both of her eyes. She had surrendered herself to the slowly blowing wind. Murat had dropped asleep on her lap. Seeing the boy's happy face, she had no heart for grieving. Just a while ago he was gulping the bagel, not obviously he dozed off out of tiredness. While gazing off into the view of the multicolored blueness of the sky and the sea, she had noticed the colors were merged and became one. She even thought about putting the boy in a corner to get up. Just in the last night Murat had woken up ill, and his face was all yellow. Thank God, the color of his face had returned to normal. Kemal had smiled at him. The smile of the man had appeared to be incomplete and broken. Again, she broke out into a sweat. Unfamiliar feelings to her were compiling for some time, and she felt like to shout at the top of her voice. Moreover, to say here I am here just to spite of your invisibility at home, and even to swear. As if that were not enough some of the swear word even the men could not dare to say…

Nesrin's husband must have had a liking for her. Just brag about it. She would tell her he most intimate bed stories without feeling a shame on her every visit. Most probably she exaggerates, and she started to assume that many stories would be a product of Nesrin's endless fantasies. How does she show off with her dried plumb-like face? Nermin was alone in bed for most of the nights. She had dreams, fragmentary, and all of them seemed to accompany her. While Kemal was sleeping like a top in one corner of the bed, strange men were entering these dreams. Even though she hasn't put lipstick and dole up herself up for a long time, some young people with their alive bodies were licking, kissing and her lips, breasts, neck and her most intimate parts, and touching her amorously. Every night a different face was entering into the bedroom of her dream. As she was feeling their hardness, she was waking up in a cold sweat, and most of the time with a feeling of as if she committed a crime. Especially their kisses. They were kind of fiery touches called French kiss. Her husband would not know about such things anyway. You, ignoble man. Keep on spreading your buttocks all night. She had sweated out so much when she got up. None of the faces of the men in her dream was resembling Kemal's. Those were not of the young state of her husband either. As if they came from the movies and became her guest. For crying out loud, did the devil enter inside of me, oh God, you are great, these were her mutterings in the nights when she woke up with repenting prayers. A sour and nauseating smell in the room. A strong odor mixed with the smell of Kemal's sweat. The window should be open to air the room. That man is somebody who would not proactive bathing after coming from work. See, Nesrin's husband has a desire for his wife ha. She queens it as she was talking about how her husband screws her.

That morning she woke up faintheartedly with bated breath. In those first years after getting Married with Kemal, in the huge parks of the city, in the places where the sun doesn't shine, he would embrace Nermin and kissed and caressed her. This woman must have appeared to the man differently with her slim waist, and colorful calico dress. There were times during those years that she had some make-up without exaggeration. How fast did it happen for both of them to get married and have children.

For some time, this trembling started, and I gasp for breath. There is an ache spreading from my belly to my lungs. There is doctor at the social insurance hospital, why don't you see him. Should I freshen up the tea? By the way, there is more cake. These are the signs of menopause, Nermin. The sky seems cloudy, and the it turned cold. The wood and coal in the stove are blazing. The conversation of two women started being cut with the intervals of silence. Could a woman experiencing menopause see such dreams, don't fly off the handless girl. Should she share those dreams with this woman? The chorus voices on the screen permeated the room. At the travel program on television – it was perhaps named as "globe-trotter" young women were kissing handsome boys in front of Eiffel Tower in Paris and having their plenty of photographs taken. She had envied them so much. She thought about the possibility of going there only after they had won the lottery. The daughter needs to get a test book. Kemal scolded the girl by saying, aren't the textbooks enough in school for your teacher. Next year, the university entry exam, courses and so on, where shall we find the money for these, who knows. On that day they had a picnic on the Prince Island. The wind was blowing gently. How happy she was that day. How much did the girl's heart sink when she snapped at Filiz that evening? All she asked was a test book. The girl is successful in school, and every year she gets com mentation from school. My dear, one should be grate full for his or her fate. By the grace of God. Go talk to her teachers, for sure they could give some ideas. Again, Nesrin slurped while drinking the tea. As you can see, things became scarce these days. Had we not owned this house, it would have been impossible to get by in this colossal city only depending Kemal's earning. Anyway, the bone with meat would not come to us. Back in the days, Kemal was like an angel. His voice used to be soft and his face used to smile very often. After so many years passed, as if he did not have anything else to say at home except asking what is there in the meal? Lately, I feel like to say to the guy, eat shit. I started developing a big grudge against him. Nermin kept on pouring her chest without being asked by the woman. As if the woman was listening to her with pity, as if she was sharing her trouble, and similar words of her neighbor including do not upset yourself, didn't ring genuine to her ear. Oh woman, I know you like a book, obviously by pitying me, you compare your state to mine, and consequently to feel happy. Her husband desires her, as it were. The boy was born the way his father. He too is secretive, slowcoach and sulky. Recently he has been getting stubborn with me. The lovebird sleeping on his perch stirred and started singing afterwards. Nesrin took out one cigarette from the cigarette box and began smoking. She took a sip joyfully from the slim-waist glass.

The men in Nermin'a dreams are hazy. In no way Kemal is attached to these dreams. At that moment, the woman on the television started to share some food recipes. Split aubergines and tomatoes and unions (dish called "İmambayıldı") should have an abundant seasoning. Really, a salah was announced a while ago, have you heard it? God rest soul, neighbor, in the end where we are heading to is certain. She pulled loosely knitted and worn cardigan at both ends. We are unfortunately not hungry and homeless. Could she ruin herself less by thinking this way? At that moment, narrowing her eyes, Nermin laughed. They say that food with tomato paste, and a woman with big hips are better. Get out of here, is that why often times so many women are on diet. Nermin's eye caught the view of the light hitting the room with its curtains open. She felt like waiting for the rain to stop at the protected part of the street, by the door threshold. The call to prayer started to rise from the mineratte. İmambayıldı, what a humorous name of a dish. To me, it sounds like a cry inside of me. An inaudible voice, a lament… After so many years, Kemal and I are now glass-eyed, and our looks are not that bright anymore. I have been noticing that my man's shoulders got narrowed and he became quite hunchbacked. When sweated out, she took out the cardigan and put it on the corner. The pit inside me is so deep, as if there is no bot tom of it. Recently, our son came inside by crying out of his beadlike black eyes. The bad boys of the neighborhood had pestered the child. They had pushed and shoved ours after a neighborhood match. He clamped up and got home covering down like his father. Likewise, Kemal button's up at the factory to his work master. That man was said to make verbal assault to Kemal at the factory. Worthless men would run their mouth off and glower at him, yet ours clamps up again, yet once home he would act as strong as a lion. Both of them would only make verbal assault to me. For sure, the boy saw it all in his father. As they say, nobility is taken after one's family, and it is the shit that smells. That day I had cut the black and curly hair by caressing, then he had stopped crying. Should she put in several more shovels? After the sky got cloudy and the sun disappeared, the rain started pouring with in large drops. Those dreams in the nights… All of them are full of holes… Regardless of her repentance in the mornings, keeping at those hazy dreams.

Again, she was lost in thought. She kind of imagined that she saw Kemal inside the crowd in front of the Eiffel tower. She smiled at him. She got closer to him. A thin hand touched on her shoulder. In daylight, both of them watched the city unknown to them. The face of the man must have come from the years of youth. The lips of the tow united together in the middle of this misty view. Nermin realized that she missed things at that moment. What were the things she missed? She missed her womanhood, maybe her youthful state. At that point, she felt that Kemal saw her at last and noticed her. Hold my hand my beauty. Let us stroll around this so-called city of lovers, whispered the man into Nermin's ear.

The dish in the pot on the fire already started to be cooked. The smell at the kitchen spread to the entire house. Should I have put the pepper paste into the dish instead of tomato paste? No, no, I am sure the salting was also okay. Hey girl, why don't you add plenty of chili powder to food. Look, there is a specialist frequently appearing on television… He also had mentioned on the last program about the fact that the chili powder is a potent aphrodisiac.

Dreams in the Pit of Hell

So many
Dead
You've got your dream
Crumb
Bum
Oruç Aruoba

17 March

Tonight the stars in the sky are few and far between. All of them are faint. The moon a full wheel.

I found out how to hate the man once I was in love with. He is hurting my buttocks while making love. I fear that he would kill me when he is on me. His lips wander on my neck, I feel nauseous, and I feel like to bellow like a wounded bull most of the time. Disgusting acidity inside my mouth. While he groans on me, I look at an empty point on the wall. He just ejaculates and fortunately collapses on one corner of the bed. There is no solution except writing my disgust and inclination to vomit at this house.

I used to scribble when I was in high school. Even my Turkish teacher used to like my compositions. Most often I used to keep my diary which I would have difficulty to hide it from my mother, in obscure places. Definitely I would have found a place the woman could not find. This would require some level of mastery. In school my literature teacher used to like my composition. I must have used the words appropriately in my writings. After many years, I felt like writing. Writing, vomiting, shouting. Heaven only knows why, this is my God's judgement, she thought about. Now I am in a position to write nothing but all of my nonsense ideas in my mind. I used to scribble hastily and secretly without being caught by my mother. Oh, those sacred hours when I stay home alone, and the boy sitting quietly in a corner and playing with his imaginary friends… Nobody comes to knock at the door of the house to chat. If only one could have friends and family members, then even the unwanted situations would have turned into something pleasing. Her husband could not be considered a true man, and he would talk to the persons coming to their door in such a bad manner and drive them away without being tactful.

I dropped out of the school through Mehmet's coercion when I was a senior in high school. Stupid me! By saying let me escape from hoe, I gradually built a life of captive for myself. On top of that, the asshole had a roving eye. Back in the days, he used to love drinking and he would have not found peace without making me set a table with drinks and appetizers at home. No those days seem to be too distant to me. Had he had not enough money, then he would pick on beer. There were times that he would zonk in the barroom two streets down, and he would be taken home flog marched. Afterwards he found the true path. Becoming a pious man, he turned into a more secretive and grumpy person. He started attending with his barroom friend the pander, Hilmi Hodja's conversation sessions. Who know how many bad ideas that man must have put into my man's head. That asshole had visited us at home for several times. In his wisdom he would rescue me from the jinnee and demons. To him, in every woman jinnee would come into being. The issue has to do to chasing them away through the husband's skill. Yours is a beautiful woman, keep this beauty away from the sinister looks of the men from the neighborhood, if you ask my opinion. He had uttered these words with such a great appetite. The disgusting man was keeping a beady eye on me. When I hinted something in that vein, Mehmet started swearing as if I flung dirt at that god-fearing man. In a way to come up with an excuse to hit at me. That night he was a pain in my backside. My multicolored dress was torn to pieces while he was pushing and shoving.

Today at home Ali kept shouted at the top of his voice. He doesn't have such a smooth affectionate attitude. I was about to give him a beating. His bones are so thin; they might get broken even if you touch them. I closed my ears and waited for some time to get him to be quiet. He went to his room crying. Somehow, he did not get used to his mother's indifference. He washed his face with cold water in the sink. He then dropped asleep in his room with his swollen under eye parts of his face out of crying.

Oh boy, we had made so much effort to have a child years ago. At that time, I had thought that maybe by having a child, I would have saved him from the barrooms and chasing women. After all he was not working on a stable job either. Debt items were piled up. We took refuge in the house in Balat after selling everything by auction. Mehmet had changed all the jewellery pinned during our wedding ceremony in order to pay the debt. Only the necklace around my neck was saved. I was hiding it from the guy for some time. My man did not prove himself to hang on to any job. I used to go hat in hand to my mother when we would be in trouble. I thought about the case if a new life would enter the household, then maybe Mehmet would change. Following one or two miscarriages in the first years, we had given hope in the child business. Either his manhood or my female feature was the culprit. My son just barely made it to get out of my belly. By pushing and shoving. If only they would know how much I suffered when he was inside of me. It would have underwhelmed as opposed to my husband's kick and beating. If it is considered love, my man tried to love me upon the birth of the boy. From time to time his eyes were becoming greenish and lit. Then he bastard returned to self. Now I have to quit over complaining about my troubles. As I was trying to keep a diary, I just started to pity my state.

This bastard never changed a bit. The girls in the high school had told me that the looks of this man reflect bad intentions. Mehmet was a short and stocky man. The girls in the class had said that you need to be careful with the person whose bums are close to the ground. My mother used to keep telling that if you are going to marry a guy, you need to make sure that his looks are genuine. This man's looks are strange, he cannot look in the eye. All of her words flew in her teeth. He assumed that it was me to cause all of his troubles. Goggling inside the house. Walking from the beginning to the end inside the house, and cursing me beginning with words of prayer for patience. I know that the boy wetted himself out of fear when he saw that my husband was breathing down my back.

Before getting married, my skin was soft, fresh, and my hair very long. I didn't tie back my hair very often. Many young boys in the high school were after me. I looked in the mirror today. I was scared when I saw myself in it. I touched my face with my hands. My eyes are blood shot. My hands are wrinkled and grew old. At one time my hands were pure white. I got withered, and obviously Mehmet is going to bury me soon.

21 March

Today I woke up with the sounds of seagulls. For some time, they flew over the roofs all day long, and shouted all at once. Their sounds resembled my boy's squeaking.

The birds inside of me always would look for a horizon to escape. I started seeing the same dream. The wolves in the middle of a mountain buried under the snow were savaging the bloodstained shirt of my son. All around seems red. I wake up in the nights in cold sweat. Again, Mehmet is fast asleep snoring.

There were times after moving into Balat to escape from the house and head for the shore. When it reached Mehmet's ears, he started locking the boy and me in the house. For months, I began to live a life of prisoner at home with the child. I found out for some time the way to live like a tower owl, far away from the eyes of the neighborhood residents. I am like a timid bird locked in a two-room house for some time.

I am far from the cats on the rockies. These cats give birth a black kitten at every turn. Each of them is poor like the bastard of the female and looked down on. I like them more than striped cats. Oh, they are my confidants, a sympathetic ear. Being far away from you makes me sad.

She can't help looking at the book frequently. I am so far away from him. As I was disgusted by my husband who paws at my body with his hairy hands, and bruises some parts of my body, I tended to keep my distance with Ali to whom I gave birth. As if my feeling of motherhood had died as soon as he was born. I barely was able to breastfeed him. Poor boy was not as valuable as those black kittens. In the beginning, he hurt me while sucking my breasts like his father did. His looks never appeared innocent; always looking at me irritated and resentfully. Still the same cunning look. I used to say to myself what was the sin of that little boy. His face is the carbon copy of his father's face.

Every night I see the same shitty dream. I keep waking up in the nights. Death is marching in my nightmares. The wolves are savaging the bloodstained dresses of the poor boy.

My husband slops up his soup, and some pieces from the soup remains on the corner of his mouth. His mouth smells always bad. Don't even get me started, that sound of his stirring the tea with the spoon at length. That sound gets amplified in my ear. He doesn't know how to kindly talk to me. Always speaking to me as if he is crashing the words. Actually, I want silence. A bit of silence.

The house was at the entrance of the street. Even the shadows of the people on the street would parade on the curtain. I was living for such a long time with the curtains closed tightly. I am only allowed to watch the transition of the season in the seven-hill city. For sure, from time to time, taking Ali with Mehmet's accompaniment, we visited the markets. Sliding door, locked. Suffocating. The darkish room. For some days, I have been looking for a lit point for me near the window.

In the evenings, I used to get into the city walls by Balat shores. Since I knew that Mehmet would be late to get home, then I would get out of the house when I would imagine that the house is walking towards me. Balat would be such a nice place in the dry cold of the night. The entire Goldenhorn would be buried under the fog. Having seen that I took the cats from the shoreline city walls' tunnels in a crazy state, and feed them with the leftovers and talk to them for hours, the neighborhood residents told Mehmet what was happening. When he got back home from the mosque, he told me that the people who were for the Friday praying warned him of why he didn't take care of his crazy wife. He was kicking the hell out of me in a rage. Devious woman, who will you have fuck you on those rockies, he started to beat her. City walls, Balat, Goldenhorn are my live memories now. The door is locked again. Mehmet went to Hilmi Hodja to have a chat. Again, they would fill his head with some crap. He started talking about bringing a second wife.

Mehmet had brought him on one occasion. Hilmi Hodja began reading the Koran at my elbow. Realizing his eyes were wandering on me, I had been furious, embarrassed and bored. He kept saying prayer, and caressing my face with his hairy hands. When the demons come to you, they should be chased away by means of faith he told me grinningly. He was trying to show his golden teeth to me as it were. Then he blew deep onto my face. My man had believed the miracle of his breath, even though that man would have fucked me in front of Mehmet, he would not object to it for sure.

23 March

When having reached the shore, I would have watched the boys playing marbles by the city walls. I used to look at the boats in different colors and lined up along the remains of the city walls. The golden horn is buried under fog. My eyes would have oriented to the opposite shore all the time. Tonight, everywhere seems to be in snow-red. Again, the same dream returned to haunt. They don't let me sleep. What they say about me, by my husband, by the neighborhood residents, and Hilmi Hodja. Gradually I started in delusion. The wolves are picking my naked body apart continuously. Two of them are howling in a rage. There is not a sound around the forest. As if they nibble at the son's flesh. I was revolted by the torn apart body of Ali at that moment. They sniffed me once or twice again. Meanwhile I half-opened my eyes slightly. I tried to move my fingers a bit. I was buried in snow deeply. None of them was touching a woman crazy like me. The blood of the poor boy was dripping from his nails. Whether it was something they disgusted my sharp nails' being a murdering weapon or else, both of them were scared of eating my flesh. I am suffocating from this damn nightmare. Now I would like to calm down. I didn't kill anyone. Or else, aren't I aware of the fact that I feed a murderer inside of me? When I was by the city walls, I couldn't help looking at the wave-less sea most of the time. From time to time though, I would have had skimmed stone on the sea during this times of escape. That was a childish indulgence making me feel good. The round ones for two and flat ones for four times at most.

Out of dirty and dim opening of the apartment building, my chocked screams are rising from time to time. They taught me how to cry subtly and leanly. People upstairs cannot hear me. I could not get out of the crying crises inside the house. Getting used to his mother's crazy state, Ali would play with his marbles and his toy cars in a corner. He even would take no notice of me. I wasn't able to live on the margins. I always was taught to be silent. Now obviously I am walking by the border of insanity. In fact, when we got married, my husband was appreciative of my being submissive and silent. As if they were wrangling words out of me. Coming near me, he would say, hey girl, talk a bit. Day by day I became much more silent. I took refuge in writing. Again, I hide my diary. Mehmet doesn't know that I keep writing.

I am only able to write my sea dreams at this house on the entrance level, where its walls are covered with spider webs. The city walls, the shore, I am both close to them, and I am far away from them as well. At times when the doors are not locked behind me, I just pay the price of my escaping through my being captive inside two rooms. Ah if only I would have been disappeared into thin air in those tunnels. If only I had hopped on one of those deserted fishing boats and sailed to different places. In fact, I didn't know how to swim. I would have drowned in the water for sure. Let it be so, maybe my cats, my confidants, my friends would have saved me. Or the sea would have protected me in its cold waters. I wanted to become confident with only cats. The poor things would not annoy me. Ah, if only these nightmares would not have sprung up. If only the neighborhood residents would have not tipped my husband about where I was, and then if only I would have been lost in those remote corners. I cannot but curse my fate.

The day I got pregnant for Ali, Mehmet wriggled himself inside of me like a snake. I didn't want him to impregnate me at that moment. He had held my hands tightly when he was on me. He was likely fantasizing to screw another woman, a prostitute when he was on me.

24 March

There are so many tunnels in this city to escape.

There is no place for me to escape.

There are plenty of tunnels under this city, Mehmet confirmed at one time. If only to reach them, I would have gone until the cisterns. There seem to be the souls of old times under the house calling on me as it were. Ceaselessly the voices reach my ear. Spooky kind of voices. Many times I searched for a hidden passage among the stones and walls of my prison.

The other day, I tried to get to the empty place behind the broken tile on the wall with my hands, as if there would be a hidden passage in the corner of the kitchen. Nothing was there except one or two dead rats. I had looked for passages so many times when the nightmare came to me and made me wake up in the nights. Since my man found a job at the municipality, he drops asleep early. Mümtaz Hodja told him that now it's our time. Don't disappoint me. My man started to beat me more as he would get rich. Thank god he fell asleep early out of exhaustion. He zonked in the bed. His snoring could be heard in the kitchen. There are no passages underground or behind the walls. All paths are sealed off to me. Once again, I caught a glimpse of raticide. I immediately put in into the kitchen cupboard in order the boy would not play with it.

Every possible place is locked at home, and the windows are closed by iron bars. There is nowhere to go. Sit the hell down. I catch myself sitting cross-legged by the window, watching the city stretching side-to-side, with attached buildings inside the fog. Several times Hilmi Hodja passed by the window. As if he ate me with his eyes. You were not able to take out the demons from inside of me. He asked about my husband. He didn't come yet, I said. Let him not miss the evening chat he cautioned. Obviously, he had been desiring me. Had I told Mehmet about it, then he would come and beat me saying that I am slandering the man he thinks is an innocent one. What a shining, magical pander man he is for the whole neighborhood residents.

As much as my man loses his head, an inexplicable feeling of pleasure settles downs inside of me. For sure, I like driving him crazy. I started not to cover my head tightly at home. I kept singing songs by turning on television. I know my man enjoys watching half-naked dancing, singing young women by looking at them out of the corner of his eye. Then he would turn off the television in a rage. They would be enough to make a Saint swear, don't watch these channels, he would tell me. As he hears that I would sing the songs of easy virtue, he would slap me in the face saying, you, godless woman. Wouldn't I know that you were after prostitutes, months ago. At which time you became a man of ethics and good manners. That bastard made me use bad language. The more he comes after me, the more I would be a big mouth. For some time, he has been beating me in the name of Allah and calling me swearing prostitute. If I am a prostitute, he must be then a pimp. When Mehmet was pushing and shoveling me I catch the misty eyed son's looks from time to time. For sure in the eyes of the child, I have nothing to be loved by him.

More and more I feel bored.

26 March

Glasses, plates, forks, remnants of the table from the breakfast. A chill came out of the woodwork in this stone building. Today I didn't feel like to clear the table. Again, the water is dripping from upstairs. Damp in the building is a trouble. For some time, I had difficulty to breathe. I can hear the rattling of the mice running here and there. Rat poison is no good. Big rats are walking under the kitchen cupboard. At one stage, I thought of killing him with rat position. What's the use of this poison on Mehmet which even doesn't kill these rats? Squeaking of the boy has been making my nerves shot. He too is uneasy like me. Recently he told me that the praying and fasting of a prostitute like you is not valid, as leaving the house. I break out into a sweat inside the house. The spider webs are driving me crazy. There is something odd in the looks of the boy. I always avoid coming eye to eye with him. As leaving the house, Mehmet had told me that he would be staying to attend the Hodja's talk, and be late. He had stared at me like an ox. There is no place for me to escape. As usual, he hurriedly locked the door behind me.

Al is playing with the plastic car in his hand in the other corner of the house. I became apprehensive about he's also turning into a degenerated person like Mehmet. Apparently, I don't want to raise another Mehmet. Nevertheless, this boy doesn't deserve such a psychopath. I just cannot touch and love this child. When hungry, I prepare some sandwiches that would make him amused, and leave them on the table. The kid got used to take his meal from there. I don't feel like to clear the table either. He would get angry for this. Today, I thought about saying fuck you. With my frozen looks, I watched the street out of the window.

I took a look at my graying hair after taking off my head scarf. There is no permission to dye it though. In a couple of years' time, I grew so much old. Until several years ago, my hair was so soft like silk. Now it is like felt. When I was a child, I had asked my mother that if there would be a bird inside of me, then would it fly there, and my mother had told me a thing or two. Don't ask me such crazy think, she scolded me. I always was a half-witted person in her eyes. She used to tell me, freak of getting married early, prostitute. She also used to visit frequently the doors of the warlock neighbors when I was in high school. Back then I used to speak to the stray cats, and feed them with the food I had stolen from the house. In school my teacher had warned my mother not to get her hands on her since she is a young girl, and then my mother had been silent for some time. Years passed since the bird inside of me had died. And what's more, like so many things Mehmet, my father, my mother had killed. Naturally, when you bear with someone like my husband, then all the beauties inside of me are destined to die.

28 March

I don't know from where did I get this idea to put rat poison into his food. He finished his dried bean dish heartily. He didn't sense any strangeness in its taste. I will just watch slowly his dying. An odd pleasure rose from inside of me. He soon fell asleep again. He said he had a stomachache. I had put just a bit of that poison. I feel like to observe his dying slowly. The women from the neighborhood were in front of the door during daytime. They would not make free with me. Back in the days they used to greet us when we went down to the market. Sister Nezahat lives in the adjacent apartment building. In the first years, she occasionally brought tome food to our house. Since I have been locked at home, she didn't stop by me.

Maybe they are grateful for their situations. At least, their husbands allow them to sit in front of the door, to eat sunflower seed, and to gossip while they themselves are not home. This is a big liberty for all of them. Please, if only they would call on a locksmith to get me out of the house. If only I would have lived through the early summer of the city and sit by the shore with my confident cats. Certainly, I would be enjoying getting wet a bit if the rain would start. I am sure the vagabonds would not mess with me in the gray darkness. If only there would be a hidden passage in some part of the house. But there are only dead rats, and muddy soil behind the walls.

So many executioners are buried under the passages in this city. Mehmet had told me about it when we moved here years ago, while he was drinking his raki. Then he told me affection- ately by saying you too could drink it. I wouldn't have seen such soft looks on this disgusting man's face. While he was talking about the executioners, those murders were visualized like a movie. I had set up my own murder plot at that moment. Their blooded hands had not saved them from being thrown into the cemetery of nameless. All of them are dead without headstones. There was no wind on that day. I feel like to leave my hair loose for some time. Even Mehmet makes me to cover my head tightly, I cannot stand it anymore. For sure, not his Allah but my Allah would allow me to disarrange my hair. The windows are still closed with thick curtains.

Mehmet has been poisoned slowly. He keeps telling me that he doesn't feel good. Yesterday, I added one tea spoon of it. Today another teaspoon. As his eyes becoming glassy, he tends to sleep. I feel the strength of the head executioners in me.

Executioners and their cruel apprentices must have tor- tured the prisoners. Mehmet is inside my dungeon now. In the middle of the night, I get up with a start. He is whimpering. Like a dead person. I can make out that the poison is spreading inside his body. He shakes all over. All in a sweat…

I looked at Mehmet fast asleep out of the corner of my

eye. My sharp nails felt the deadly power in the hands they belong to. I watched him in disgust and the feeling of nause-ating. He would not get up even you make the loudest noise beside him. The poison pervaded all parts of his body like a snake. He keeps being all in a sweat, and talking in his sleep. When I got on him and put my hands around his neck, I felt the power of those head executioners whose stories I listened to in my hands. Even though while half asleep, he made efforts to get rid of my hands from his neck, my nails acted like a sharp knife and caused him to bleed in streams out of his neck. I watched his dead body with pleasure. My nightie was all in red and blood. I went on watching the night after opening the window. The moon was up.

I came around by Ali's crying. Thinking that he must be hungry, I prepared a sandwich in the kitchen for the boy. I left it on the table for him to take it from there. My hands are in Mehmet's blood. When I turned on the faucet, I noticed that the water was accumulated in the sink. Now it is a red-hot pond.

I have to feed the cats by the city walls. I filled whatever food remnants were at the kitchen into a small pot. The poor black kittens and my striped brothers and sisters are waiting for me.

The night is of a sparkling sky. That is to say, there is no fog this night over the Goldenhorn.

The Missing in the Photograph

I

*I am catching the sight of the date at the back of the pho-
tograph: 23 April 1982, Sivas, 4 September, Park. My mother,
myself and my elder brother. The machine caught the steps of
the woman in the photograph. As if the look of the woman was
decided by the orders of the man who pressed the shutter. I guess
it was my father to took the photo. In fact, he was the one in
our family history to take every photo frame. My eyes are at the
back, lost in some unapparent point. I was 5 years old. This time
around, am examining the photo from the perspective of the other. Outside, the sky is being encircled by grayness while the sun is
trying to add color to his paleness through its weak light.*

A boy with blond hair, a madcap curly one, his hands are
inside the pocket of this pants, one step back from the mother
and his elder brother. Elder brother is wearing a pair of velvet
pants, and a striped sweater, and he is around ten. Following
the 23 April ceremony, they took a walk all together. One of
the frequent strolls taken in the family history.

The memory residue hidden in the photograph made its
mark as such in my mind. The remaining is only the residue,
I gather. I am turning to a second photograph. It must be
Antakya. Three persons are sitting in the balcony. Again, the
mother, the elder brother and the younger brother. The father
is also missing in this photo frame. April 1981. The machine
froze the time one year earlier than the first photo. They are
indulging in the early spring of the Mediterranean in the balcony of the house. An exhausted woman. You can read it from
her face. With her long sleeved and patterned shirt, and the
pair of horrible house slippers, exactly as it is at home. With
no frills. Her looks reached the machine half-way, she is pretty
contemplative. The younger brother, with his small body, having settled on this tiny stool, is watching this beautiful woman
in admiration.

I am studying the features of the women as I am holding the photograph in my hand. With the longing for not having seen her, my fingers wander on the photograph. I notice the ridges and roughness on the photograph. I caress the white and pure face. I really would have likened this woman to Belgin Doruk for many years. I associate it to one of the Yeşilçam movies for a moment. The cameraman is shooting her bitter and absentminded looks. Ayhan Işık will show up soon.

When you are over thirty, it is quite difficult to think of a distant memory. All of them have their indistinctive marks. I am really in bad with the pains of the adulthood. Most of the time, what remained from the childhood years seems to be a burden to me. This time around, remembering that this woman died in the car in which I was also a passenger, is hurting me. I have spent so many years without her by joking about so-called death. I think of the photographs; the ones she is in them. The last photos which still have their marks in my mind are the ones belonging to my high school years. These frames keep her face and her motherly attitude alive in one of the corners of my mind.

Throughout my high school years, I used to get back home with the school shuttle. During the rush hour in İzmir in the evenings, there would be a traffic jam, and a painful wait for all the students in the shuttle minibuses would start. She would be waiting for me at home, and if I would be a little bit late, then she would become agitated. In my every opening the door with a crash, she would be waiting for me with an affectionate smile by the door. For every boy who is less grown, with a childish soul, returning home would be like going back to the venter. As soon as the door is opened, then I would give her a big hug most of the time. Once I had told her that I would be going to university in another city, since I had to hatch out, I wanted her to free me. In fact, her love was not one of the suffocating and destructive. When I broke my decision, she looked sad. She had listened to me calmly though. As if she was waiting for my decision to flee. She tried to conceal her feelings. Grief was accumulated inside of her. Seeing her son flee she watched for, her son she did not let leave her side had scared her a lot. This was so because my elder brother's studying out of town. She didn't want to have his other son going to faraway places. And what is more, she knows that the navel cord between mother and son is cut during these age periods.

II

The photographs harbor non-natural smiles, made up life joy, makeshift affection pervades the frames most of the time. In the photos of my mother, myself and my elder brother, there are traces of the forced migration from one city to another over the years. We were eventually two children who heavily footed the bill for 80s. Two sons of Selman Hodja, going to the same junior high school. My elder brother was caught drawing hammer and sickle in his notebook when he was in the third grade of the junior high school. We are waiting in the school yard regimen tally. While the students with their ties are dropped, the upper buttons of their shirts are unbuttoned are taken to a corner and the classes were being herded inside, the sulky deputy principal takes a look at me in a rage. Following his words of "Hammer and sickle ha, you are Utkun's brother, aren't you?" which reflects his anger on his face, a big ruler descended on my palm. I am paying for the hammer and sickle in my elder brother's notebook, as we had been paying for my father's being the union president.

We are in Maraş. We had get to the land of my mother as if we were fleeing Sivas exile. In the first years of the junior high school, nationalist and religious conservative teachers are always on my back. My mother and father are angry for the pressure we were exposed at school, yet this is the anger only to be articulated at home. The children should be rescued from this city, both of them were repeatedly saying. In fact, we had left behind an exile when we got to this city. I am in the prep class. I watch "Uncle so and so" on the black & white television. He is talking about executions, what the military did for the country and nation as well as the country which turned into a bloodbath prior to the coup. His sentences sound affectionate; at my age this man seems to be a fairy tale hero. I am growing at this age with the fairy tales for adults. As I was watching the "From Within the Action" of the uncle with a darling face, what was told by Adile Naşit becomes alive. My father and mother do rarely turn on the television for their exhaustion of getting bored of watching pashas and darling uncles on the screen of the television. Books are being read more frequently than ever at home. After a while my hand touches the huge bookcase in the living room. Party colored books of all sizes in the bookshelves. Each of them seems to be unfamiliar to me at the beginning. The books of Sait Faik, Orhan Kemal, Nazım Hikmet lay together. In every move, these books are boxed. The workers who carry these boxes to the truck are cursing in anger. Turning to my father, is there the corpse of a donkey inside, they say. It's time for reading books with my mother. I have known Yaşar Kemal, Aziz Nesin for years. During my reading hours with my mother, her sentences about the writers and books are peaceful. At every occasion of book reading, it is to be discussed and evaluated. The books would readily become a tool for a magical game. She doesn't judge the books. As she didn't judge my father for his share of being exiled from one city to another. That's why I started loving this woman for this reason from those years on.

III

Most of the time, I relive Maraş with its sections which had suffocated me... My grandma teaches me how to perform

prayer. There would be a prayer oral exam in the small classroom converted into a masjid at the Anatolian High School. My
grandma is a woman who doesn't miss praying performances
and doesn't leave the house without putting on her abaya. The
poor woman took pains to teach her grandson how to perform
an ablution, to start saying a prayer first reciting bismillah. In
fact, to her, I was a stubborn grandchild who barely put up
with two week Koran course, and not being able to memorize
surahs. Actually, she was acting like a calm teacher when she
was trying to teach me. She doesn't seem at all like the culture
of religion teacher trying to sell tickets to heaven. In a rush to
cook the dish in the kitchen, my mother is watching us with a
desire to believe what is it exists. I don't like Maraş. The land
of mother is suffocating. The mental picture I have include,
the scent of musk pervading the downtown, the market crowd
of bearded men and women wearing abaya, and my frequent-
ing the religious bookstores upon the insistence of the science
teacher. This time around, my mother and farther didn't want
to waste their children in the countryside towns. In a couple of
years' time, they are appointed to İzmir. In every photograph
my mother and father took, a wide and bright smile settled.
Now I am in a new school.

*I unbuttoned the upper button of my school shirt, and loos-
ened my tie at my new school. Teacher were not making me
afraid. There are no deputy principle herding students to the
classrooms holding a ruler in their hand. I can breathe.*

IV

Beginning with my childhood, I would like to browse
through the family albums. The secretive and dreamy stories
could be explored at the dull looks. My mother is at my elbow.
Telling me the stories of many relatives of whose name I forgot turned into short-length film in my mind. "This is your
brother's wife, by her side is your grandma." "Here you were

one month old. We had bathed you with your grandma in the bathtub." At first I was ashamed with the nakedness of the baby in the photo when it was taken at the age of two months. It was considered strange by my mother for a moment that her son, who connected him to life through the umbilical cord, now blushing with shame at the age of fifteen in front of his mother. She knew that I was growing, moreover as if breaking away. She had smiled at that point. Calm and peaceful one. Now she is glancing at the album. She is looking at my father's face in the photo taken ten years ago in a romantic way. The eldest son of an Alawite family from Antakya loved a Sunni woman from Maraş who was also working at the same school. The elderly of the two sides had not consented to this marriage at first. My father even broke the engagement with a daughter of a family from Antakya in order to marry my mother. Yielding to my father's stubbornness, they had the two get married. After many years, my grandmother from my mother side would have taken this brown-skinned and slim boy to her bosom like her own son. Throughout the years, with this brown skinned boy and the white and fine faced woman always harboring a smokescreen in her eyes would have been in a position to toil to make their persistent love live in their age of twenty. They would have not wanted to let the so-called marriage's strict, blinding features turning into a habit enter into their life. Or maybe I would like to remember those days as such.

– You had a narrow escape, says our family friend. The car had turned into a file of iron, and it would be a miracle to have someone get out of it alive, according to his explanation. Get well wishes come next.

Itching suavely created by the neck protector and necessity of having a rest is causing me qualms.

– How are my mother and father doing?

I don't understand why I wasn't taken home. Following the accident, I was brought to the family friends' house in Antakya at a moment's notice.

My aunt's husband tells me that my mother's situation is serious and still in the intensive care unit. The following day, when they come with my aunt, the quieter and distressed looks on their faces. They are preparing me for the black-hearted news. My father has serious broken bones, staying home. A fear of losing grows inside of me. I am thinking of the woman going and coming between death and life at the intensive care unit. Every passing day, my questions are being evaded and avoided. My elder brother had stopped by while I was asleep. Following the accident, he had come back from Adana hurriedly.

The accident comes alive in my mind piece by piece. Getting tired of being nomads by spending their holidays in a tent, my mother and father had bought a modest house in Çeşme with their retirement grants. We were on our way at the early hours in the morning of the holiday to see the house. The roads were empty and the weather was rainy. My father was driving the car. Selman, the car is skidding, watch out, we are skidding, then the car the car rolled over. Period. I was at the hospital.

I do recall the moaning of my father at the hospital, or was it my mother's? While I was being taken out of the rolled over and banged up car in a heartbreaking fashion, my mother's words were printed on my mind: let the boy be taken out first. Or is it something I do remember a dream?

One week later, the son of the family friends, of the same age as me, tells me the truth with his reserved and teary-eyed face. The reality is merciless, for a week though, the people who visited the house had been preparing us for the bad news.

– They were not able to save your mother. They held a funeral yesterday. Your mother was buried in the family graveyard in Antakya. It was something unexpected, not being able to confirm, and exploring being an orphan. I had cried for hours forever and ever. A couple of days later I am going home with joyless steps, my elder brother is on my side. We are walking weakened and helpless.

The door of the house is opened. My aunts are in front of me with their tired eyes. A heavy and strong smell of medication. Every detail in the house is a reminder of a hospital.

– Did you come my son?

I am scared of taking a look at the room. I answer the question of the man lying motionless in the bed and his body with fractures all over unenthusiastically.

– Here I am father.

Countless medicine bottles on the night table by the bed. Those drugs alleviate the pain of my father confined to bed for fifty days. For weeks, my aunts are mobilized and give his medicine to him and feed my father with liquid food. On the other hand, I locked myself in my room. In order not to lose, it's better to plunge into dreaming and live with dreams.

In the nights, the groaning of my father reaches into my ears. I have difficulty in sleeping; I have to sleep though. I have to get rid of the burden of thinking about death. The things I see in my dreams are fragmentary. There is my mother inside those dreams. Every evening, at the door of the house there is a knock. The one at the door does not ring the bell. A persistent sound. There is nobody else at home except me. When I opened the door, the woman in front of me says, I came. I don't ask where you were. I just embrace her as much as I want. I grasp her body as if I am being embedded in a soft pillow filled with cotton. She becomes one of the family photographs in the family album in my every hugging. Her face is though in the whiteness of a corpse. Cold and pale. The dream is interrupted, and I wake up in a cold sweat.

We are in Antakya. My elder brother and myself. We are walking along the pathway stretching from the village to Harbiye. My father is a couple of steps ahead of us. Grumbling, my grandma is plucking gillyflowers and begonias lined up along the road. Her sentences are in repetition, ya veylah, ya meşkin. Poor kids, she says in her language. We arrive in the cemetery on the slope of the village. We take our steps in silence, and in fear of wasting the words. My grandma put on the hose in the tap of the charities of the cemetery. The headstone is yet to be erected. She begins to water the grave surrounded by the tiles. The prayers in Arabic is being read one after another. She pays her respect for the woman she did not feel anything in the name of love, by sobbing.

I am dreaming of my mother's body by the grave. Brown-haired, white skinned, having gained a few more kilos, a beautiful woman. This time around, the images in my mind are being replaced. A grave with nothing but a pile of bones eaten by insects. We are carefully place the myrtle twigs, begonias by two sides of the grave.

Our silence gets cut suddenly. Three of us go through a crying crisis with groaning. We are sharing our being orphaned by the grave, my father from his wife, my elder brother and I from my mother. After a while our hiccups die away. We don't want to grind one another with our common pain.

We are on our way returning from the cemetery. We are going down the pathway by slow steps. There should be a life after death, I say to my elder brother. I would like to believe in a utopia. By taking up my mother's simple faith attitude, I dream of my mother watching us from the other county. We had decorated the grave with flowers in different colors, vibrant flowers. The grave full of cypress trees was blowing gently.

At the turnout to the village, my grandma had jumped in a heated conversation with one of the women in the village. I catch their looks full of pity. I glance away from them.

My father, myself and my elder brother proceed along the roadside. This time around, my father is included in the photo frame.

The One without a Shore

I just don't have anything to say, here is my face, here is the
night
The silence of memories in my voice
Haydar Ergülen

Moving on the pier, he walks towards the lights standing crosswise the Haldun Taner building. He catches the glimpse of the crowd surging from the bus stops to the pavement. The red light is doggedly on. Everyone is in a patient less waiting mood. Grunting ones, the ones having not enough sleep are lined before the light with their bloodshot eyes. At the moment when traffic comes to a halt, a few people from the rows run across the road. The others wait sheepishly and silent. There is a feeling of submission in the crowd he is also a part of it. Somehow the red light would turn into a green one, and the mechanical voice would change. Now you can cross.

When the traffic lights indicated the green, he reaches the market without hitting the bodies crossing the road from both right and left sides. The ugly and multi-story attached buildings are line up along the streets of Kadıköy stretching down the sea. It would be good to have a cup of coffee without sugar at one of the coffee store. Coffee and cigarette. He considers them as two bosom friends. His exhaustion seems to invade his body; his steps are shaky.

Immediately after the stores, bookstores, on the gaps cutting the cobblestoned street of the market, musicians had installed themselves. They sing songs in different languages, the tunes accompanied by the instruments of the tambour, the guitar, the tambourine are being heard. The sun seems to be able to show off itself with the light breeze of the spring. It slaps his face gently, not too strong. This year the spring came late. He would not like the winter from his earlier recollection. The screams of the seagulls reach his ears, each and every one of them is shouting at each other flocky over the fishing boats. His steps are becoming sparse as he was walking inside the market. The café houses in the marketplace had already put chairs and tables. His eyes catch the vies of the young people buried in their seats. Hurried, anxious, and incomplete sentences of each and every one of them seem to be fallen down the street. He thinks, it's time to enjoy the spring. As the poet says, it is such a sunny and calm street to make one to submit his or her resignation from the office of the foundations.

Along the shore on the other side of the market place, the commercial and public boats are waiting for him. At least he wants it to be just like that. We shall see the beautiful days, children, we shall sail the boats to the blues, it is possible to go to another harbor. One of the boats by the seashore would take him, maybe it's possible to find a remote corner. First it would be good to have a coffee without sugar, he thinks he could tell his fortunes. He wants to predict his fortune by examining the coffee grounds.

The familiar keeper of the coffeehouse invites him in. In his mind though, there is that boat waiting at the pier. First the pleasure of coffee, the route he would take would be hidden in the coffee grounds in the coffee cup. The captain of the boat is going to ask him, where to go, "Nowhere." His coffeehouse keeper friend, someone from the acting circle, invites him to a table in the sun. A coffee without sugar, as always, he enters inside with a teasing smile on his face. He lights the cigarette he took out of the box. The blue flame of the lighter burns first peevishly, then calmly. When he inhales the smoke, a tang is felt inside his mouth. His eye catches the view of the tray on which there are coffee, water and a piece of Turkish delight. Today you are absentminded says his coffee shop keeper friend. When he is on board of the boat, he runs into the beaten face of the captain. The captain had already started the engine, to take him to his "Nowhere". The seagulls are accompanying them, and for a while the boat moves forward towards the light blue horizon alongside with the flight of the seagulls descended upon the dead fish by the shore some time ago. The seaweed doesn't smell. The eyes of the two are lost on the point of the horizon. Every detail to remind of the city, such as buildings, attached streets, bus stops is not visible. By coming close to the stern of the boat, and leaning his back on the jetty, he gazes off into the view of the infinite blueness. The night lights of the city are lost somewhere over there. The full moon is accompanying the trip.

He composes himself with the flickering smile of the coffee shop keeper. He makes the last sip of the coffee trail inside his mouth. He sweetens his mouth with the piece of the Turkish delight. He catches sight of the coffee grounds. His coffeehouse keeper friend invites people passing by on the street using some agile gesturing movements. He finds the words quite unnecessary at that point. A good number of tourists are already convinced through his mastery coming from his acting career. The tourist group of men and woman had already settled down on the empty stools.

"There are a couple of good plays at Haldun Taner this season." After a momentary pause, he replies the coffee shop keeper's question.

"Sure good plays, but still each of them is going to be performed the way they were staged ten years ago." He goes towards the tourist group at the other table with his endorsing looks.

For a moment, he catches the joyless and suspicious look of the shopkeeper enjoying himself in front of the antique shop at the end of the street, at several costumers browsing through the small statues and vases. He slowly approaches the man touching the statures. In his mind, he imagines to sell it with too much high a price tag.

"Tomorrow evening there is the play called the *Sour Cherry*." He says he watched it last month. For some time, he doesn't feel like neither a movie, nor a play. He just gets off works, idles around the market place, getting lost among the books for one or two hours. Leaving the book stores, he finishes his shopping. Most of the time he gets back home without being late. This monotony gradually must have turned into a habit.

He skims through the coffee grounds. He tries to interpret the images on the coffee grounds as if he was a soothsayer. You got bored. This road leads you to contentment. Can you see the sea, there a boat is waiting for you to take you to the other shore? When the coffee shop keeper realizes that his eyes were buried in the coffee grounds, he teases him for a moment, "Oh, are you reading your own fortune?"

Bored of his absence and not having a friend for hours, his cat is waiting for him at the door. As soon as he opens the door, an hour long meowing ceremony is going to start. It is not hungry; its food is still in the bowl. This is the way the animal curses for being alone at home for hours in the cat language.

He sees the boat waiting for him on the residue of the thin coffee grounds. The ones who would set off on a journey, far seas are wavy and combative. For a moment, he is afraid of getting the boat to capsize.

There is not much to reach the shore, says captain. You should know that the sea here is wild. The expression of tiredness on the face of the captain wanes. Now he is smiling broadly. What will you do here without a city and people? He is bewildered by the wise question of the man. This is the best option for Nowhere. The darkness of the evening descends on the shore, the shadows are falling on the oak and beech trees stretching along the mountains. After a while both of them become a shadow. He extends the flashlight to him, "You will need it." If he would be alone in this pitch dark, then this flash-light should be used. "There is an old hut by the shore, there is there a few things you might need, and they would be suffi-cient for you at least for couple of weeks." The darkness might eat up his mind, and for a moment he gets scared. He thinks that at least he would manage to spend the night with a weak light. What else he might need by this shore except the books, draft short stories, the notebook which he always carries with him, and a couple of dresses he had put in his backpack?

He moves forward with wobbling steps in the darkening of the evening. "You are alone in this solitude; the vast sea is now yours." says the captain when he prepares the boat for the return. After a while he heard the noise of the engine, and the boat drifted apart chugging. The boat was already going astern. As the boat was moving away from the shore, he lost his looks in the eerie stretch of the forest. A starry night. "I was lost in thought on the coffee grounds." On the face of the coffee shop kept, there is a desire harbored to make sense of what he saw on the coffee grounds. Apparently, you found a shore for yourself to go, the eyes of the two were casting an eye on the coffee grounds. "Who knows?" he replies with a shy smile, be-ing apprehensive about his secret trip's being exposed.

He waits at the distant dark spot of the night. His eyes are searching a road along the pathway illuminated by the full moon. He tries to spot the dark vegetation through the flashlight. He reaches the pathway fast by the hut. He becomes a point now. A lone and silent point.

Without a Story

The mobile phone is ringing insistently. I couldn't recognize the number on the screen of the telephone. When I picked up the phone, a soft and an anxious voice asked about how I was. I was not familiar with that voice. However, his sentences were as warm as speaking to someone you knew. Let us meet, he says. Why don't you come to Galata? We would drink something near the tower. At this hour of the evening, even I catch the last boat, I would get to Galata only in an hour's time. I remember you like Bomonti. We would buy a couple of bottles and settle on the stairs of the apartment building. The Saturday evening, bars and barrooms are crammed. Whey I would like to go out even though the voice is not familiar with whom I make plans to meet? Maybe the thought of having drinks on the street must have been attractive. I think that when we come face to face, then we would find subjects to talked about. A young boy in his twenties, his voice gave his youth away.

I need to remember his face, then we could explore each other's thoughts. One hour later, he is going to wait for me at the exit of the Tunnel. Dressing up swiftly, I wash my face down and dirty. By giving a rough shape to my hair in the mirror, I start moving towards the pier. How he knows that I like Bomonti, in fact I prefer red wine. I wouldn't want to drink it in the middle of the street. Had he known all the details about me, then his voice would have not been this much strange for sure. A couple of hours ago, it rained madly. First the sky got delirious then became calm. The rain water had filled the dry places under the soffits with small dots. After a while, the softly drizzling rain stops quickly. When I get to the street, there I get dressed by a domicile weather. I will catch the last boat to depart from Kadıköy. Karaköy in the evening hours and Galata in my mind. The sound of the noisy tourist group has invaded the boat with their laughter. I was startled when I was going down to Karaköy from Haydarpaşa. The seagulls are flying to follow us. Now the Galata Tower must be bursting at the seams. I have been having a poor appetite for a couple of days. When the boat birthed in Karaköy, I tried to stand up by rubbing my knees which were weakened out of hunger and frailness. The voice on the phone tells me he is waiting at the Tunnel. I notice that the mosquito that shot full of holes all night long. The disgusting mosquitos had flown busily all over my ears throughout the night. I had bloodshot eyes because of the lack of sleep. All day long, I moved about the house like a lost soul. Cursing the mosquitos flying all day long with an insatiable appetite, hey sting me if you like, I said to them. In the end, I went on sleeping to have dreams, and left the light on. When birthed in Karaköy, the passengers started to get to the pier one by one. I have to reach the Tunnel via Bankalar Streets. A sparkling street. I am passing through the magnificent apartment buildings built a hundred years ago. These buildings used to be the arteries of the commercial life of the city. The dense odor of the dead fish thrown by the fisherman of Karaköy from their stalls is making my nose tingle.

I move toward the Tunnel following a tourist couple in the boat. I climb up along the cobblestone road. He was supposed to wait at the last stop of the tramway. He must have get there already. I don't remember his face, and I have just some incomplete traces in mind regarding our meeting. We had a long discussion about our identities during the Living Library event. It was one of the vibrant books about the identities the society doesn't have much affectionate feelings. He was answering the questions of the participants with irony. He had told the participants sitting in their chairs, I am a gay. His purpose was to mock them with the insulting and sharp-tongued words. As if provoking the curious looks sitting on the chairs, he asked if you have questions about this gay book? Throughout the event he kept facing off the repulsive and twofaced ethics of the society, and querying the common ethics in terms of finding out whose ethics it is.

He is waiting at the bus stop. He greets me with an affectionate smile. Your eyes are bloodshot he said first similar to his previous sarcasm. We are walking towards the Tower. Both of us maintain our silence of not calling each other and meeting together. This time around, we are descending on the road, on which I had climbed before. Could we find a dry corner of the stairs after the rain? There was no rain on this side, he said smiling. Only an army of big clouds are hung in the sky. First, we could not find a place to seat on the street. Corners, stairs, every points reaching to the Tower are being occupied by a crowd of men and women sipping their beers. Laughter, humming noise are streaming along the street. We come across a snack shack on the street across the Tower. We buy two bottles of beer. One is of Bomonti, the other one is the dark beer. We immediately coil ourselves up on the stairs of an office block with its external gate is locked. He doesn't have intention to tell, to talk at first. Our eyes catch the glimpse of the Genoese architectural structure. There is a timid and wild expression in his eyes. Why he wanted to meet, I don't want to answer. He called and said, let's have drink.

Our looks have to be intersected and met. Whereas his and my eyes are taking a glance at the Tower's walls.

– I think you are a student. At our last meeting, you had told me that you were a freshman.

– Cinema, but this year I suspended study. I barely put up with the private university for two years. On top of that, this is the second university.

I have to listen to his story. If our bodies come side by side, then our words too should come across. He was a slim, silent boy sitting beside me. At least, as opposed to his wild looks, I had framed his personality he expressed in this way. He doesn't know where to start talking. His first sentences stumble, and his speech flows following in complete sentences.

We are among the people who got out of the event, now sitting at Asmalimescit. I have to recall. I am upset about my absentmindedness and his powerful memory. He lives on Ömer Hayyam with a roommate who came to Istanbul from Denmark as part of a student exchange program. They rented two rooms six months ago. They live at the same building with the landlord. Living side by side with the landlord is not an easy thing to cope with, he says. He has been here in Istanbul since his high school years. He had stayed at state dormitories for many years. He had spent his five years in the crowded rooms, where six people were using the rooms of fifteen square meters, in between bunks. Cutting in on my talk, there is a beach under these pavements he says. I have difficulty now to decode his sentence not connected to his previous words. Let it be so, throughout the event, he was trying to add and philosophical dimension to his speaking out of turn. When he told during the event that nobody has a right on their own bodies, I took a note like industrious students. In my mind, for a moment, the beach under the pavements be comes alive. After he had read the *Ones Who Couldn't Hold On*, he kept a distance from books. The wisdom residue in his every word seems to be a bit bookish to me. All of the words he uses are well-chosen, pompous and bigger than his age. They even sound uninspired to me.

You have been in Istanbul for thirteen years, he says. His smiteful face goes off the boil for a moment. A joyless and anger-less look embraces his face. He drinks beer one after another continuously. He tells me that he is envious of me having a stable job though he is not much fan of being a teacher. During the first years of the university education, he had learnt all the jobs half measure without having a permanent career, according to what he had to say. Three month for being a bartender four months for the souvenir shop, and six months for being a voluntary translator for the festivals. In his life, working has always been something on and off and as messed up as his life. I am a gay not being able to concentrate on life, he says by mocking himself. On that day, he had called the participants who were sitting on the stools as the Ones Who Couldn't Hold On. He was constantly referring to the only book he had read up to his twenty. Since we were down to sit on the stairs, and by having hidden the things about myself I wanted to tell, I had preferred to listen to him. Silent and timid at the beginning, the boy got rid of his uneasiness, he was telling everything about his life as is he was talking to himself. Even the most disturbing details were also inserted into what he had to say.

– On one occasion, I had sex for money.

His travesty neighbor at Ömer Hayyam had mediated his meeting with the man. He wanted to find out the inner world of a male prostitute by going through this experience. In the first year of the university, when he was short of money, he experimented it out of curiosity. He considered himself as a subject of a social experiment. He was a kind, naive and a bit shy man. He had some pleasure too, he says. The man's descending upon him and groaning had first turned into a love making. He even turned the man's touches in a hurry into a bit slow moves. I wanted him to enjoy my nakedness, he explains.

Afterwards he wanted to sleep naked by embracing him. Putting his arms over the chest of the boy, the man had gone into sleep a wild smile on his face.

– While he was asleep, I kept thinking without blinking an eye. When I got up in the morning, there was a bundle of money on the coffee table. I didn't feel like doing it one more time.

The confusion on my face doesn't give away any trace of disapproval. Once he gets that I wasn't judging, he keeps expressing his sentences at ease. As I distinguish every emphasis, every secret punctuation, I gather that I am a good listener.

Since high school, alone in this city while living in Trabzon, his mother and father think that it is enough to ask after him from time to time. After a while, he comes to know to live alone, and to stand on his own feet.

– This year I will transfer into the design department of the university.

At some hour of the night, we are being forced to leave our spot upon the warning of the police. We are walking along the Istiklal Street down to Cihangir Park. I didn't think that one bottle of beer would eliminate the troubles in my mind, and how quickly we are now half-tipsy. With this state of soul, we could wait until dawn and drink. Descending down from Galatasaray, we are moving toward Cihangir Park.

With their roommates they started to hunt apartments in the neighborhood of Harbiye. They are sick and tired of the heated fight between the landlord and his lover, even leaving their dirty dishes to them to wash. The last straw came when the unnecessary warning notes stuck on the dishwasher put by the daughter of the landlord. After buying two bottles of beer at Füruzağa, we are going down to Cihangir Park. Along the stairs, among the pieces of the broken bottles and sluggard looks, we are hiding in one of the corners opposite to the Peninsula. The Peninsula carries a unique spell under the night lights. The Topkapı Palace, The Blue Mosque, The Hagia Sofia seem gloomy to our eyes in the soft yellow color of the artificial city lights. Their shadows are fallen in the water. We are sipping our beers, and our gazes are lost on the opposite shore. At one point, loneliness is a fate of a gay, he says. His eyes are fixed at the reflection of the water at the Peninsula. If only he knew that the fate of all of us happens to be loneliness regardless of our age and our being gay. I attribute it to his being immature.

– Do you think can I make a story hero?

– What kind of story hero?

– Genuine, flesh and blood, just an alive one. It should be explained without making it dramatic though.

My wish to listen to, to analyze him, turns into a desire to read what's there in his mind. Everyone could be a story hero, and even the most mediocre lives are worth of being told. Through furtive glances I am trying to reach the boy who accumulated so many experiences in life until the age of twenty. Our conversation would not be all eye to eye throughout the night. His eyes are stuck in the void. The following day he is going to apply for a job. He dreams of creating the fabric shoppers by his own design at his simple workshop he set up in his room, and selling them.

– Shall we shoot off. He says what we both think of. We are walking towards the square. The remoteness of the night has fallen in Cihangir. His silent looks are lost again.

– I wanted to tell. There are occasions I share them with others too. Maybe there would be some people who would like to write.

I gather that he is in bad with writing, and he is contented with only being a narrator. We are proceeding with weary
steps.

I say to myself, who knows. I fathom that I had already
constructed the backbone of the story.

An Ode to the Water

"God who embellished the world is still inside this universe; yet humans don't know how to look for and find. Tough the fish are inside the sea, yet they don't know about the sea"
Hayâlî

Arif and I were hanging about by the cost-line at the dead hours of the evening. We had skipped school. We had taken out our shirts from our pants, and we had chucked our jackets into our backpacks which already went bad. We had decided to pull a cork by sitting under the rocks. Let us catch fish he said. We had placed the beer cans into a big nylon bag, and bought two fishing rods from the shop by the beach. When we got to the rocks he started to smoke. He handed in the cigarette, why don't you drag, he said. I don't want to smoke, I replied timidly. What a mama's boy you are he exclaimed sarcastically. Here the blue fish would swarm at these hours. We had placed baits in the needles on the tip of the fishing line, and thrown our fishing lines into the sea. With every movement of the fishing line in the water, and in a childish happiness, we were waiting for the shoal of fish visiting the bait. As we were sipping our beers, our minds were falling apart, we were getting lost at the dark horizon point in our eyes. Gathering courage, I wanted to take a drag from Arif's cigarette. He extended the cigarette by calling me tag tail. We have started to dream under the light of the flashlight in our smoky night. Our eyes were staring into the water with the weak illumination provided by the flashlight at the cape.

"Again, the litterateur called over the coals» I said as I dragged one more smoke from the cigarette. With all his indifference, «Fuck it» he said. We were lightheaded. Seeing every move of the fishing line was a shot in the arm, and we were standing up by hasty movement. A couple of times, we pulled the fishing line swiftly. Except the small fish, they were not visiting our fishing line. Apparently the fish didn't have appetite this evening. They will be waiting at home, I talked in whisper. He shushed me through his stern gaze. His mother was used to his coming home late, and she wouldn't say anything when he would open the door creakily early in the morning. «Today my babies sent these blue fish» she said with a smile. The freight wagons coming slowly from afar were cutting our words. "Your father is an asshole dude» he inserted while the train whistle was doggedly blowing. I kept quiet. He knew that my father got home last night as drunk as a skunk. My father had walked up to me in a rage like in the previous nights, and whaled away at me by saying «Stupid, are you going to study the same class twice!». I collapsed. His hard hits fell down on my cringed body. When he saw my pitiful state, he had cursed more and kicked my belly. My teeth had clenched as I tried to protect my body. With his shrunk shoulders and glassy eyes, this pathetic man would turn into a monster if he drinks one or two glass of alcohol. In fact, I would find the sticky smile settling on his face in his jolly times, and his laughter accompanied by salivating unbearable.

He had turned a deaf ear to my mother's hopeless calls, and I had to take refuge in the corner of the room with the smack of his huge hairy hand fell on my face.

Being unable to slow down, the monster turned to my mother this time. As he was walking up to her, he was evading my mother's begging by uttering profane language. I attempted to wipe the blood coming from my nose in a thin streak form with unsteady touch of my hands. My mother was crying bend double at the corner of the sofa. Listening to what I had to tell, Arif repeated in a rage and fires burning in his eyes, "Asshole!" "I will fail the class at this rate" I said. I wanted obstinately to make him forget about the pitch battles at home. In fact, we didn't care much about the school and classes. Both of us were hardly passing our grades anyhow. Except the pander literature teacher, we were not considered screaming at anyone. As a soul, we were breathing in the class. We were not messing with anyone, and we were just taking refuge at our desks going into a deep sleep most of the time. The teachers would not interfere with us. With all of his self-indulgence, Suat had raised his voice and told them to fuck off. He remained silent to my mulish effort to change the subject. Lighting his cigarette, he took a drag from a cigarette. At that moment, he coughed interruptedly.

I had retired into my shell.

– Had I stabbed that bastard, we would have got rid of one scumbags, then me and my mother would have been freed.

He did not budge and inch. He listened pensively to me with glassy looks.

– Did the fire hit your head, man. Who do you think would watch for the softhearted like you in jail. Get rid of these nonsense in your head.

I kept quiet. My malignant dream of my father's beating me to death when I get home, snapping at me to say where did you get the flashlight go dead, went away with the smoke of our cigarette. Arif, with a pure heart would know that I would not murder even an ant. I would have not interfered with two legged bastards either. After a while, I was as quiet as a mouse by his side. Our eyes got lost in silence which was felt as an eternity.

"Most of the time, I feel like to get on this boat and go away, when I come here" said Arif. We both were lonely like the fish, being in the sea but not knowing about it. His eyes couldn't help looking at the boat by the shore. "Where are you going?" I asked smiling. Two crazy ones sitting side by side lost ourselves in the faraway darkness. In his every tipsy moment, Arif would feel like to escape. He would board on a boat for some time, and on a transatlantic for other to go faraway places. "There would be a place to go" he assured with a soft voice. Our thoughts were disrupted by our fishing rods moving with a stir in the water. The more I was pulling the rod, the deeper the fishing line going down in the water. "What an obstinate fish it is" I said. A big blue fish, getting tired of its stubbornness, got out of the water by hitting the rocks. The stubborn fish was struggling. Arif meticulously took out the needle from its mouth. "Well done to us, such a big fish of the sea" he cried with pleasure.

Arif's fishing rod started to shake. We waited for a while to get the shoal of the fish to take the bait. "You are lucky" I told Arif. He looked at my face wonderingly. "Dude, it is called mastery" he claimed when the fish were out of the water still struggling. He shook the fishing rod once or twice. This boy was lucky. His father had gone to Germany two years ago to work in one of the big factories. He would visit the town once a year during his off days. He would live a happy life with his mother. He would not see the nightmares in the nights where the howling drunkard fathers take part. Her mother would not get pissed off at Arif being late to get home most of the time, and his coming home dead drunk. She would be sad, but she would live her sorrow inside of her. She wouldn't say a word to him anyway. Even though she would pull a long face a bit, then with a big kiss placed on her cheek by his son, usually she would be consoled. At that moment, a wide, and bright smile would appear on the face of the woman waiting for his son restlessly, sleeplessly.

Apparently, a huge shoal of the fish had attacked the bait on the fishing line. Arif stubbornness and the resistance of the fish not to get out of the water reminded me of the pitch battles told by the history teacher in glowing terms. The big blue fish hit the rocks by moving in the air. Looking joyfully for a while at the blue fish swinging hanged on a branch like ripe fruits triumphantly, Arif took out the needles from the fish. "These are so good for grilling" he said in high spirits as he was sipping his beer. "Should we bought a couple of more beer?" he wondered noticing that the bag was gradually getting empty. He and I noticed the unopened can beers in the bag. I didn't feel like sleeping bent over on the rocks by sleeping it off. "Give me a drag" I inquired pointing out to the cigarette between his fingers. "Dude, you became a true bum. You see, I guess we are going to rotate this damn thing all night." as he extended his half smoked cigarette. "It would have been better if we roast all of them in this crackling fire and tuck in." At that point, his looks got lost in the blinding darkness of the night. Our looks were stuck in the reflection of the moon like a plate. His eye caught the view of the boat tied to the rocks. His books became unstuck with the whistle of the last mail train. Unenthusiastically he dragged again from his cigarette. My eyes were stuck at the struggling of the blue fish inside the bucket. As if they were looking at me with their bulging eyes. Such strange creatures they are, I said to myself. For a moment, I envied the blue fish that couldn't escape the wrath of their batterer, drunkard fathers.

In one move, we came near the boat, and holding on to the oars, we settled ourselves in one corner of the boat. "Let us drink to fathers" Arif sat when he took out a beer can from the bag. In confusion, "To which fathers?" I asked him. The words "Cheers!" raised in the twilight of the night with the beer cans in our hands. Our cheers were so much laden with alcohol though.

– To the ones who don't flee dude, he said. His face faded out a lot in the starry night.

My voice was raised in a pathetic tone.

– To the ones who would not beat anyone calling the son of bitch, I shouted. The screaming of my voice made me startled. For a moment, I heard the echo of my cursing voice. My face got a fever-like color. Could they hear us from the opposite shore, I thought that the echo of my voice got lost in the in-finite water. We were quiet. We were shrunk up inside the boat, as if getting smaller and smaller.

Inside the boat, Arif was staring at the sparkling eyes. "One should flee" he uttered following the broken sentences. His ev-ery word was reflecting his being lightheaded. Those words were describing his getting to Germany from the Danube river banks by means of boarding on a ship, and the Cologne streets of which his father was singing the praise. In the smoke of his cigarette, the spotlessly clean Cologne streets, blond, white-skinned women with plumb and lively breasts came alive. He placed himself in one of the corners of the smoke.

While listening to Arif, my gaze reached the slowing down moves of the fish in the bucket. What my grandpa told me came around in my mind. To my grandpa, once the fish was taken out of the water, then it would be doomed. Even though you throw them into the water, their life would be short. Still, nobody should have been cut from their uterus. I stormed out of the blocks and emptied the bucket. We needed to give a change to these poor creatures in our pathetic lives deserving to be beaten. While doing it, I was being afraid of their angry and monstrous looks. The blue fish just were just poured in the water. If a funeral for them to be held, then it should be in the water they are used to be in. His astonishment cut with coughing had turned into a big laughter. Our eyes caught the view of the fish fallen in the boat. "There only remains this single fish, you see," he said while drinking the last sip of the beer in the can.

The fish had drawn its last breath and was staring at us with its glassy eyes. We had to go back. It wasn't a good idea to sleep here bent double. The cold wind licked off our face. Fearing the falling down into the deep sleep in this corner, I stood up at one swoop.

The light of the flashlight fell down on the road. Arif had moved away already. His moves were slow to be deemed as awkward. I watched his departure with a timid smiling. He is swinging that single fish in his hand. In seven minutes he would be at the station, and in ten minutes he would get home. And for sure again he would console his mother by placing kisses on her cheek. It's not worth bearing the sinister face of my father at this hour. I was silent, there was no fight or noise in my mind. Yet I had to get back home. Had I not returned, then my father would be taking revenge from my mother. An agonizing ache in my had, a nausea in my stomach. I had vomit, I had to throw what was inside of me by retching. I quickened my steps in order to keep going. I hesitated for a second, and I spitted while I was passing by the shrubs. My phlegm got lost in dark. Still I felt like throwing up what was inside of me. The disgusting face of my father, my mother's tears she sent inside of her while cowering in a corner, Arif's looking for his father in Cologne's streets, and swaying about, his mother's waiting for his son out of the window of their one room house, and the cursing looks of the literature teacher... I threw them out by roaring out and letting the tears of the river flow from my eyes.

I returned. I am waiting for the light at the head of the street going down the sea illuminating the boat. Getting home would take a long time. At least five minute, I am too lazy to do so. I got bored of this road. I am alone on the road stretching alongside with the sweetgum trees. My father is angry, and again most likely he would have my mother to lock the door.

No Life

They were on the boat. The sun is about to set. The horizon is red hot. Across the Sultanahmet, the Hagia Sofia. It resembles the cities in the fairy tale book the teacher in the elementary school forcefully made us read. Two of them are in the open part of the boat. The elder sister and her brother had batted around all the streets. By lowering down from her shoulder, the girl placed the accordion beside her brother. They went on watching the seagulls, the sea and the big city. The girl's eyes caught the newspaper laying by her side. One of those with many pictures. It was left there after having been read. A news about a murder. Her step father ran amok and killed their step daughter of sixteen shooting by his service pistol. The girl's dead and cold body is laid at full length on the bed, with her glassy eyes. Her eyes were stuck at the photo in the newspaper. All of the stepfathers should be burned in hell. Putting woods under the colossal caldrons, each and every one of them should be burned. The boat is about to berth in Kadıköy. The boy is gazing at the seagulls and the sea. He is in a fa r away place as opposed to the storm inside the girl.

When they got out of the Karaköy boat, the area was bursting at the seams. It was best to get to Kadıköy Market Place. Both of them took a look at the sparklingly lit showcases of the stores. After a while they settled on the pavement of the crowded street. The pavement is cold, the weather is grey, the clouds are motionless. The girl lit a cigarette, drew a deep breath, one more time…

Her eye caught the sight of the showcase across the street. The seven years old boy looked at his elder sister with hair in plaits. There was an imperceptible admiration in his book. Her mother tied back the girl's hair forcefully. "If you don't tidy you and your hair, then you look like a prostitute" she told her with an affectionless touch. Her mother hurt the daughter while she was tying back her hair. Her elder sister carefully placed her accordion on one corner of the pavement. She was looking with still and empty eyes at the showcase. A long and ceaseless look. The multicolored, latest fashion dresses were being exhibited in the showcase. Checkered dresses, blouses, sweaters appeared more magical under the lights in the show case. She threw a look at the box filled with cash money. In the box, there was about fifty lira worth of money at most. She thought that the strappy dress in the showcase would go well with her. One liras, fifty kurushes, five lira banknote thrown into the box by a middle aged man in the boat who tweaked on her cheek. Both of them were hungry. While waiting on the pavement, the boy agonized at having his hunger pangs, got closer to his elder sister. Why they didn't have a feast of buying a meatball and bread using a bit of the money in the box, and even an ayran would go well with that.

"Sis, I am hungry."

"Just wait, don't be impatient. We will eat soon."

The eyes of the elder sister were on the yellow floral dress in the showcase. She put on that dress on her weak legs, and skinny body inside her mind. Though it was not looking as good as it was on the mannequin. Again her eyes oriented towards the changes in the box. She thought that the step father at home would be angry at her even five or ten liras would be short in the end. She was startled by the pitying looks of the several people passing by.

"Hey, let us not be idle around. Let us play it here."

Feeling her way, she held the accordion and placed it on her legs, and started playing. Maybe five or ten more liras they might make on this street. Her fingers wandered on the accordion's keys. Several people got closer to them by lending an ear to the song being played, and watched the girl curiously. They threw the change they took out of their pockets into the box held by the boy. The boy's heart was still on that meatball and bread. The girl's looks seemed frozen and the pavement felt like ice. The harsh northeaster of the city had also started. The boy shivered slightly. He was trying to conceal that he was feeling cold. He would button up for everything, and he would never make a noise about something. The wind chilled him to the bone under his t-shirt. Three young people when lent an ear to the familiar tone of the song were watching two of them curiously. Already a small crowd was formed around them. The fingers of the girl were wandering on the keys of accordion she placed on her spindle shanks. This was the way she memorized and repeated action. Three years ago, her mother was told that "he is a good man, for how long you are going to grieve over your husband, let us get you to marry." "He was supposed to be the father of two children." The woman had accepted to marry the drunk coffee shop keeper of the neighborhood upon too much in distance. Then the man moved in the house like an illness. She was resenting her mother for a long time. Finding a husband was such a nonsense. She found the trouble instead. For three years without delay, he made her prepare a drinking bout, and drank until getting dead drunk. Then all of a sudden he would lose his temper and getting angry with the people in the coffeehouse, the men on television, the woman singing in the clip, and the commercials in between programs… Using a pretext, he would whale away her mother. Most of the time though, two children at home would receive their share of violence. She used top lot to kill this man shouting loudly, going crazy, and pressing the girl on his big and burly body on his good days, laughing loosely. The murder case news passed through her mind she read in the newspaper. Had she killed her step father, she thought, then she would take the murdered girl's revenge.

Some money would enter the house; the man had said. Even though the woman insisted that "She is still small, she has to go to school" yet, she was not able to convince the man. She is not into a school or class, her head is in the clouds, so they had her drop out of school after finishing the first grade of the junior high school. Her schoolbag was put away in the cupboard, and her books were given to a neighbor's daughter going to the lower grade. The girl having six bad marks in her school report did not object to be taken from school and was rubbing your hands with glee, as it were. Her mother was not surprised that her crazy daughter accepted to play the accordion on the streets all day long. She had taken after her father regarding involvement with the musical instruments, adulterous behavior, unmanageableness. Putting the accordion over her shoulder and walking the streets was rescuing the girl from the suffocating environment of the house. She had learned how to play it from her birth father. Even at the age of six, following her father, they would stride through the same streets, and she would watch the accordion playing man in admiration, and she would get enthusiastic with the change thrown into the money box in her hand. The girl didn't know to read the notes, just playing by ear. To his father, she should play as it would come from her soul, actually if a person has a musical ear, then it was not difficult to play. His father had the pleasure of teaching her as she was walking his fingers on the keys of the accordion of which she was hardly carrying on her small body. In a very short time, she learnt how to play. Had they not beaten her father at the exit of the barroom, then what business it would be for that man to be in their house? Yes, her father too would drink, yet he would not beat them. He would get drunk by being aware of loving his two children.

The house was suffocating her. And the house was smelling mold and alcohol. Loveless-ness had pervaded the four walls.

Early on, she was leaving the house in haste, her small brother by her side. The hustling and bustling streets of the city, and the city lines boats belonged to them. With the songs she was playing, she had won over in a couple of days' time, such a considerable amount of audience members.

Her step father had thought about getting her married when she would reach the age of fourteen. Since the woman knew the craziness of ill-temperament of her daughter, she hardly had her husband to change his mind. By saying, this child with her farting by her side would not bring trouble to her husband.

The tunes risen from the accordion spread throughout the whole street for a while, but faded away soon after. The people on the street were watching the girl as if they were applauding. Two siblings noticed that the box was full to the bream. At least they made money to suffice for their meal. She took a look at the tips of her toes having formed a crust like the old women. The accordion was like something entrusted to her for a while, and she was sick and tired of mugging for all the world. As she was playing, she felt the same misery by the circus animals when they were thrown fruits to them from behind the cage. The sky is starry; stars are visible up there. But until a couple hours earlier, it was a dirty yellow scene.

Her daughter has been a headache for her mother. Since

the very beginning, she didn't give her consent to the marriage of her mother. She didn't have the toleration for her mother's happiness. Slut was expecting from her mother to grieve throughout her entire life. The man actually is good. A husband should watch for his wife and children. The boy and the girl were not hungry or homeless. If he would be drinking one of two glass of alcohol, what bad is with it? Her late husband to would come home dead drunk. At least this man would know how to come home. The neighborhood folks used to collect the late husband from the streets. Her mother thought that jinee and demons entered inside of this girl. As if they took her from school forcefully. She was so happy when she dropped out of school. Yes, the guy is heavy-handed, and she was beaten by him many times, yet he was protecting his house. From time to time the girl was being slapped by her stepfather when he was drunk. Let her know how to become an obedient girl. This girl's looks are weird. She was getting mad at her cold and secretive way of behaving. If you let her do what she wants to do, then she will sleep on the street with her brother. We should pour lead on this girl to repel evil eye. The girl squinted, she is looking at the man as if she would kill the man. She thought of her daughter's birth. The pain was so violent in the night of her birth, she had caused great distress to her even she was in the womb. When she took on her lap, she couldn't warm up to this swarthy and skinny baby.

Two days ago, two of them returned home early. The man was in good spirits, her mother cooked the dishes, they would eat as a family. At one corner of the table, her stepfather moved his raki glass in his palm. He stared at the girl. He grinned at his wife by opening his mouth with some missing teeth. He was as happy as a sand boy by saying "Look, how nice they work, and some money comes come". The girl's gaze was in a rage, and she looked at the man's body which was full of fat and hunched in disgust. Again, he tweaked on her cheek, and placed a kiss with lots of saliva on her cheek. Her mother was full of beans. This man was being the father of them, if only she would not be a nasty piece of work. It was in vain when she talked to her, do not upset the man, please him. The girl's face seems to be as hard as it might become. This girl must have taken after her late husband. It is for sure that she got her bad temper and viraginity from her drunkard uncle.

Her fingers wandering on the keys of the accordion got tired of playing the same song. The street got emptied up one side and down the other. Here and there people were walking around lit streets, and the stores were getting closed one by one. The girl felt nausea out of starvation. When turned to see her brother, she caught sight of his tired and silent looks. A soft smile appeared on the face of the boy. The small boy must be made happy, and they should have the meatball feast at the restaurant on the corner, coming with ayran. She put down the accordion on the pavement. She wanted to make herself present able. She tried to pull the dress which was sown by her mother from calico, and now gone bad, at both ends. They were going to have a feast. She needed to get rid of her hair in plaits resembling the girls going to elementary school. She dropped her pitch-black hair over her shoulder. What a relief! Let her mother, the prostitute would say something. She got up with a relaxing feeling inside. The boy was following her. By putting the accordion over her shoulder, she walked towards the restaurant.

The girl lighted one more cigarette. She took a drag, and was revolted by its tang. She coughed right after the second drag. A gray cloud was settled in the darkness of the night. Going through the deserted remote streets they proceeded between make-shift shanty houses. The cars were passing on the asphalt road speeding. The street where their house is located was in dust and dirt. Trash pieces were being scattered through the wind from the bags shot to pieces by cats. The laundry hung at the balconies of several houses were fluttering by the southwester. The September evening would be harsh. A dead calm weather of several days earlier dropped off the map. The girl was pensive and worried. The boy was walking several steps ahead. Incompatible with her elder sister's slow steps, he was hurrying up once in a while. Her elder sister made him stop in a rage. What's the point in hurrying?

When taking to the street where the house was, they saw the piled up tiles and paintless houses. All of them were crooked like her legs. The house on the corner was their house. A house without a roof, just a naked house top. Today the troubles of the street didn't show off. The high school dropped boys of the neighborhood had started messing with the girl for a week. "Freak!", "Male Fatma!", "Hey girl, do you have breasts" were echoing inside her ears. Vagrants of the neighborhood would like to mess with the girl. When she opened her mouth, she would swear like a trooper at every time they went at her. The street is desolate. The boys must have been looking for their trouble on other streets already.

He was there too, two nights before. Finding a distant place on the corner of the street, they were drinking their beers, and making a lot of noise. The boy's looks were meek without a rage like in the others. When she caught the furtive look of the boy, the girl felt something weird. He was a slim, tall and cute boy. He was in the next four class in the elementary school. There were times that they played ball together on several occasions. The boys told that the girls had nothing to do with football. But when they realized that that the girl was dribbling fast in the clay field, and her command of the ball, they had to say, "let her play" in astonishment. The boy had grown taller in three years' time. His childish manners were gone and now he turned into a brave young man. As the others were messing with her, he acted to restrain them, he was telling the boys in a rage, do not touch the girl. There was an angel on the face of this crazy boy, looking at the girl with a soft smile. For a while, she searched for the boy's looks on the empty street.

Her brother opened the gate of the garden of the house. Both took a look at the unplastered and naked house. Drawing their house was an extremely easy task. As effortless as drawing a stick man. From the flowerpots placed by her mother at the bottom of the wall covered with tiles on top, the scents of violets and chrysanthemums were spreading out. Penetrating and heavy. The lights of the one story shanty house were off. The guy must have pegged out, and her mother too would be asleep. She thought of the knife she was hiding under the pillow. If her mother did not enter her room, then it must be there for sure. She opened the door of the house slowly. The eyes of the two siblings caught the glimpse of the table a couple of steps beyond the door. An empty seventy cc bottle was on it. Besides that, there were half eaten appetizers. All night he must have drunk using up. She got angry. Evidently the bastard made a fuss. As if it was not enough for her mother to be beaten by him, she must have carried that eighty kilos animal to the bed. She felt happy that she had no blood relation to that bastard.

When entered the room, she started shivering, evidently the stove in the house was put out hours ago. Two beds on the ground facing one another were at their usual place. This small house was smelling moldy. Dampness was everywhere. The boy wanted to bury himself under the blanket and got to sleep immediately. A long and un interrupted sleep. She turned on the light. She felt the cold coming from the corners of the window chilling to the bone. Having the boy put on his pair of pajamas, she kissed him on his cheek. Rolling in the blanket, the boy tried to warm up. He immediately fell asleep. The girl's chin clicked. Her mother's putting the double layered newspaper by the corners of the window was not helping much. Her hand reached the beneath her pillow. Yes, it was there where she had left. She relaxed. Her eyes caught sight of the pair of pajamas by bed's side. She got undressed hurriedly and put on her pair of pajamas. She recalled that her brother holding a box in his hand, following her to tour with his sister on all streets of the city. She remembered the fairy tale of the Pied Piper of Hamelin. Her father had told her about it when she was five. They were walking from street to street carrying the accordion in her hand. But there were no mice coming from behind. She also recollected that in this evening that middle aged man on the boat who squeezed five liras into the box was almost screwing her with his eyes. She touched her small breasts with her hands. She got that she didn't want to become a woman. She should have stayed as a small child, away from all the burdens, from all types of big troubles. She buried her head into the pillow, and the hairy blanket visited the corners of her mouth, and her back trembled, her teeth were set on edge at that moment. She didn't want to be the mother of any child to be impregnated in side of her body. Not even the mother of the children who were condemned to have their step fathers… She wanted to sleep for the dream giving peace by those soft pillows. She was warmed up. Her hand touched the refuge of the insecure sleeps of the night, yes it was there.

It must have been a nightmare. There was a weight on her, not allowing her to breathe. Her step father was flying on her, taking off the girl's sweatpants by one of his hands, and caressing her legs with the other. He was hurting the girl's legs with her big fingers. "Don't be off your rocker girl" he said groaning. She felt his hardness on her panties. Though she wanted to escape from the body of that big and burly man, she disgusted so much, she was not able to do so. On her face, his rotten smelling breath was wandering. She was nauseated, and wanted to vomit. Her brother was in a dead sleep on a corner, he would not get up even there would be a shooting. "Stop girl, crazy slut" he was saying when his hands were exploring inside her panties. She remembered what was beneath the pillow. Her hand stretched there. The knife was in the air through a sudden move. The girl started to see red. This must have been one of the dreams in which she was plotting a murder. She stabbed the knife one more time. The bastard was groaning but his groaning was light. She wanted to get rid of the animal on her, and feared that she would be smashed under him.

The blood, very dark, blood clot... The dark malignancy bleeding from the back of the man had created a pond on the bed cover. The asshole was groaning, and both his hands and body started trembling. She was being pressed under the giant body of the man. Had she screamed, everything would have turned. She barely wriggled out of the trembling body of the guy. Her step father was toppled over the corner of the bed. The girl loathed the blood stained on her pajamas. Silence filled the room. The step father was lying motionless on the bed. She wanted to take out the knife on the back of the man. There was an inexplicable relief inside of her. The smell of blood reached her nose. She felt that she got rid of one burden, one trouble. This feeling was like a door leading to an inner serenity. She didn't want to think of the calamity the dead might entangle her in. What could have changed more in her shitty life? He must have kicked the bucket. The man was looking around with empty eyes, as it were. Since the cold was oozing from the window, she started shivering. She should leave the house. She pulled out a jumper from the closet near the bed, and put it on. She could not leave her brother. She should wake him up. For a while, she looked at the body of the bastard which started to get cold. Her step father's eyes lost in emptiness reminded her of the looks of the girl in the photo she had seen in the morning in the newspaper.

Messenger of the Storm

A balmy wind in the Mount Amanos blows during the scorching heat in the summer. The roosters crow out of boredom all night long. The village houses are lined between large gardens. Is he my grandpa? Alone. As old as a melancholic Ümmü Gülsüm song, his beard is graying. Every summer he expects that his grandchildren would fill the village house with their merry voices. He is looking daggers at my grandma. This is the rage he is not able to get rid of from her heart. Retiring into his room, he would get lost among his books. His voice is heard by the black & white photo in the room. Sons, daughters, a house where at the loom bed sheets are continuously woven. His young eyes are sparkling. He would not lament for what is the past. He planted the pomegranate tree that year. Nar means abundance. I bought one in the market, it became one thousand when I got home. Habibü'l Neccar (Hatay) was very green back then. The city was not yet settled on the skirt of the mountain with all its being patched-together.

– When is your school going to be finished, my son? My grandpa asked.

– What do you study? My grandma wondered. Literature I said. The woman muttered that it was not much use unless you become a doctor, and engineer. My grandpa appreciates poetry. He just asked me if I would read poetry after the school is finished. One of my uncle is an engineer, and the other uncle is a doctor. I on the other hand, am a teacher candidate, the son of the teacher. When I brought the Yunus Divan's facsimile, his eyes had sparkled. This gift of his grandchild was precious, indispensable la for this man who could read the Koran fluently, and who would know how to write in old script.

My grandpa had fortunetelling ability with an affinity to hurufism. The journey of the fortune telling would start with names, the letters, and the Koran verses. He was the first man to consult with in case anyone in the village would lose his or her valuable articles. His forespeak would be most of the time right on the nail because of his prediction and largely his knowledge about his fellow villagers. This man, with his eyes getting lost in depths at the blissful gathering of raki without anis, has always meant to be a mysterious wise person to me.

– Don't you see it kills you, day by day, my grandma said mixing Arabic and Turkish. She put her raki glass on the table in the garden by cursing. Beside the skim-milk cheese and humus she took out of the fridge. My grandpa didn't say a word. This woman didn't like him. She had given birth twelve children from him. Two of them had died even before being born. She had hated more with every child she gave birth. She would constantly find fault with every bed sheet this man weaved although he was the man who brought the silk fabric weaving to this village. She was unable to make head or tail of a drunkard's impeccable workmanship. But he was not one of those men who would be howling. When he drank a lot, this man would turn into a calm and introvert lunatic.

He dragged me to his corner. His graying beard touched my cheek. He smiled. At that moment, I noticed that the color of his eyes was laurel.

– Are you going to be a teacher now?

– Yes grandpa.

– Like your father ha. Learn Arabic too in school, right!

– There are courses about the Ottoman Turkish, but they don't teach Arabic grandpa. Maybe he was upset because of my response, a feeling of sadness descended on his eyes for he didn't teach his grandson his mother tongue.

The large garden of the house in the village. Trees of sloe, walnut, laurel and pomegranate. I had planted this pomegranate tree when you were born. I wanted that it would herald abundance. He had wanted that the first born grandchildren would bring fertility to the soil, and the children who would be born should be able to run in the emerald green garden. The weather is calm. We sleep under the mosquito net in the nights. Each of them would go through the mosquito net. My grandpa is in his room, in his corner. To me, that corner was a treasure chamber in those years. Cassette tapes, books, black & white photos. The heat is suffocating. In fact, this weather is a messenger of the storm. The all saints' summer of the Mediterranean holds some unexpected storms. During the day, my grandma is running in the garden. Grumbling at the same time. Again she is collecting the ripe plumbs. Soon, she would gather the silk cocoons from the boiling cauldron with a ladle drenched in perspiration. Crisp and clean silk shirts, sheets will emerge from the weaving machines. My grandpa is calmly enjoying his drinking raki without anis he drank during the day. His eyes are at the threads on the machines. It is not an artisanship but what he does is an art. He would weave the sheets like poetry, my father keeps saying. Every bed sheet stands out.

Pomegranates ripened, about to crack.

The river Asi's water was cut off. Syria cut off the water, they say. It's not good even we take refuge in shade. The heat is a killer. The village was drowned by the smokes. A fire broke in the Habibü'l Neccar Mountains. They couldn't put out the fire. Good old shrubs, trees of oak and pine perished all day long. It tore my grandpa's heart out. He became more quiet. He wanted to be invisible. He drank again. His body got used to drinking a seventy cc bottle. His eyes got lost at the terrace of the house. His eyes caught the glimpse of the pith black, bald hills. He carried the cassette player to the terrace. Ümmü Gülsüm had sung for hours. He cried. His tears touched even my grandma deeply. Despite her intolerant heart, the woman was saddened by the lament in Arabic recited by my grandpa for the dying trees. She grumbled behind her. With the desire to keep the rage alive in her, don't you see, it kills you, day by day, she said.

– Are you too going to be a literary man after you finish school? He asked when he took away his eyes from the bald hills. He wanted to wipe his tears. Maybe he was told that the grandfathers would not cry. Like they say, fathers don't cry. He embraced his grandchild, and he couldn't help looking at the pomegranate tree in the garden. Yes, it was there. He was pleased.

My litterateur grandpa was a man worth of his name. One of his side is against the established rules. He was not a Sunni nor an Alawite among all the devout grandfathers of the village. We believe in our creations, he said when we took a look at the bald hills. We would also cry for what we destroyed. I listened to his lament in Arabic by his side. Ah, if only I would learn his language and I could understand fully the words of his lament.

"the days passed….
the days passed
as distant and pained ."[1]

---

1 Ümmü Gülsüm, "Daaret El Eyyam (Days Passed)"

Death approached him slowly. He drank his last glass with pleasure. He walked in the garden taking steps slowly. The governor made a statement on television. Habibü'l Neccar would be reforested. The River Asi is calm again. The storm stopped hours ago. The laurel scent spread in the garden. The pomegranates were already ripened. The seeds inside should taste sweet now. The fig trees called out and listened to the gryllidae in the garden. Every summer they all make noise. He made the walnut inside his palm circle around. Everyone at home was asleep, and the mosquitos are in charge now. He cursed saying bloodsuckers. The hands of my grandpa turned very green because of the walnut shell. It will become brown a bit later. It would stay on his hands for a month. He looked at his very thin and dead hands. One month was too long. All day, his grandchildren ran about around the pool. He felt proud of being a grandpa. Then he retired to his room. He said his last lament. Gülsüm's soft voice on the cassette player. A smile on his face. He wished that the green on his palms would turned into brown. There was no time any longer.

My grandma shed tears for the death of her husband. What made encircled her heart was the pain of losing her enemy. Death had approached her in that room. In the following morning a storm broke. Kind of storm plucking up by the root of the trees.

Pomegranate fell down on the ground. The seeds were scattered on the soil...

Associative

I have to write. Even in such a way as if throwing out my rage. Parallel, there is a thief, hey what's going on in this country… It's just about vomiting. Her lips touched mine. You forgot to love, I will teach you loving. Touching. I am getting USED to get up every morning with you. You know I am not a fan of habits. Hey bro, they would cover this robbery up as well. The protesting children shouted there is a thief. Each of them is either at his seventeen or eighteen. The body should not get used to the country. There is indigestion for days. The drugs are no use. I think I love its smell. Calling you my love, though you don't need to be long to me. If only we would learn by heart how to become us. All of the religions are born depending on lie, oppression, and rage, then becoming brothers. In case we become brothers. Do not let our feelings narcotized with opium. I am used to my silent, cool four walls. The street is crowded, and all of those multistory mushroomed buildings are monotonous. Side to side, the window of somebody else, windows of other by it, the curtains are drawn. They return to their houses at dead hours. If only we would be purified from our hopeless loneliness. Loneliness derived from being simple.

Blending is maybe to get complicated. We are naked, apparently the dresses are the caves me take refuge. Whose ethics is the public morality? There is a tumor in my brain. The neighborhood, the city knitted that tumor. Slowly, without being in a hurry, they knitted every one of them. My brain, the spider web of the brain. First blind ness, then insensibility.

"Good morning." I got up with you again. Last night our shadow was reflected on the wall. Two big heads. One those heads is crocked. We were puffing on. The light is dim, maybe the room was dark. The moon had entered the room. I kissed you. You embraced me. I am here, you had said. Did I fear that you would run away? The country smells, how about my body? Maybe sweat. All day long, we shouted slogans together. We beat the pavement of Kadıköy. We commemorated those kid killed by state violence. You smiled at me at the marching cortege. Where are you my love. I am here my love. By your side. Following the press statement, we drank tea. On the antiquarian street. A strong tea for each. Do you know, I am as lonely as Sait Faik? The island, birds, fish were not aware of his deep and wise loneliness. In fact, I always find my being secludedness quite foolish. We walked until the house, let us prepare something at home this evening. You gushed over my salad, chicken saute. But I don't know to make food. I did put everything into the pot and cooked, that was it. Fortunately, I did not poison you. Following the wine and the movie. We didn't watch the news, willfully. Nonsense is flowing on the screen, lies, angry statements, makeshift optimism. The headlines made you curse, we might as well like the movie. Utopian world, fictional reality. All of those realities became banal. Let us design the uncertain one called the future on the utopian track. What are we, you wondered. Your bringing to book pleased me. Habits. Apparently, I was placing people around my corners in a kludgy way. My cat curled up into a ball. He slept with us all night. He also included you in his life. First night you told that he was the first cat you were able to touch. Your eyes were pure, my reflection on the brown of your pupil of the eye. I grew old. Under eye sections, do no lie. One should be honest with the mirrors.

Which antidepressant I have been using for years made the passing time bearable? I become a slowcoach and weakened body when I take that medication. You attributed my silence to my gentle character. Whereas I was on the other side. I hid the drugs in a distant corner, and I didn't want you to see them. It is unjust to expect from you to love a lunatic. I have no idea, to what you ascribed my insomnia. I walk through the forest of dreams only for one or two hours. I move away in fear, it's spooky. Angry grumbling, unrest of the birds. The shadows encircled the forest, dark and black. I got up all in a sweat. A peaceful smile on your face, it is nice to see you happy by my side. Teach me how to be happy with myself. Bro, this country will not change. The thief watch for the thief. They would fabricate shoe boxes to hide shoe boxes this time around.

Doctor, I have the problem of indigestion, the antidepressants are not enough. How would you tolerate this smell? The streets smell corpse. The young people without breathing, cats. They are all condemned to be rotten in the trash cans. The flies gathered around dead bodies. Vultures, carrion lovers. THE FLESH GETS ROTTEN, THE WATER TOO. I am holding Beauvoir's book "A Silent Death". The writer described his mother's dying without a fear or apprehension. What would you say my love if we explain our annihilation? You are affected by life, last evening you got angry with Tezer Özlü. In order to write about a suicide, you don't need to try it, you said. Do you receive the smell, which smell? My body, there won't be a funeral for it. There would be no prayer for it. Don't let them to hold a religious ceremonial pray reading session. The living dead would go silently. Even you would not notice my absence. Actually we have not met with you.

The street smells. It's not urine. The rotten flesh. There is a thief, the city is blind and deaf. The drug boxes are empty. I didn't throw any of them away. The sky is starry; I have NO LIFE. The ones who don't live cannot talk. Their cheeks shrink, under eye sections rotten. My white, pale face. We have never met. I would have liked to meet you somewhere. Maybe at a bookstore. Look, Walter Benjamin. Woolf is by your side. They had not forgotten Zweig. All the late writers are side by side.

"Everything happened. Place me on top of the woods that would burn the dead, the feast is over."[2]

I threw out, you can find my puke in the municipal waste yard. First I got cold, then I started to rotten. The sky is sunny, countless stars. The ones on the ground would see the night better. The cold would not penetrate the rotten flesh.

"Good morning. Do you know, I died last night? It was one of the showiest suicides."

"You forgot, we died together last night. They forgot us in a vault. You know, the dead would not lose their consciousness.[3] Skip it, let us sleep my love."

Did we really get rotten?

---

2 Last word of Robert E. Howard. **Edgar Allen Poe, The Pit and the Pendelum.

Gnawers

He slowly perched by my side. That makeshift smile on his face. By touching my shoulder, he uttered a few words asking about how my day went.

"You are depleting my soul. You have been gnawing me since you entered inside of me. Where did my inner voice come out, they have made me crazy for some time. Every moment I assume that I quit interpreting life with negativity, you are after me. Ah that burden of suspicion! You again encircled me from all sides. I cannot breathe, do you get it? I need to be without you. Two persons in one body is too much now."

His looks, the amateurish sincerity at his touch on my shoulder startled me. His call was way out of frankness. As if he was not someone who would appear by my side at every moment, and who would always be judging. Why don't you have this tea without slurping. You eat too fast. Don't even get me started on your smacking the soup… Among all the states of loveless-ness, these affectionate situations happened to bother me already. He apparently loves to play. For years, I have envied his success in the play of acting as if loving without loving. From the time you became me on, I was not able to digest you anyway.

The shapeless body in the mirror, crooked nose, hollow face, dull eyes… There was a bloodbath outside again, he said. An eastern wise person said that the geography is your fate.

Isn't it always like that? He made his face bleed while shaving. He cursed his being clumsy. Your shirt is un ironed today too. You look like rascally with these wrinkled dresses.

His eyes caught sight of the sinister looks of the voice, controlling his life. For some time, he turned a deaf ear to what he had to say. The same intonation, the same words…

Cliché. This should be the familiar word regarding the monotonousness of the days he's having. Yet he would not like the repetitions. He on the other hand was repeating everything. As he was complaining about the slack ness of his steps, unorderliness of his face, the simplicity of his story, he noticed that he was also acting the same way. He was like one of those talkative literary critics. The narration of this life, its editing, the depthless of the characters didn't fit well. There would be no book out of these elements. Just a life without description and soul, just an uninspired life. Moreover, it pretty much a carbon copy.

The first lights of the morning. The sun reached the entire room. There was not a spot on his face for a shade. Yet what he wanted was a shade. If only there would be a shade. He looked for a place for himself on the web at the ceiling a spider spinning. He thought of his hands and his body were inside an invisible web. One or two signs of haste and resistance. There is no way to escape. In that case, enjoy your captivity. Being gnawed every day is not hurting you though.

He rode in all directions inside the house. Outside is crowded, he dreaded. Riding on the metrobus, he would stand up and spot a place to breathe. It would be better if he stands by the corner of the window rough-and-tumble. At least, he would enjoy the panoramic tour of the city. How about the inner voice, drink me? If only he would not fit into the metrobus. He is so big, fat and ugly… Again he doesn't feel like leaving the house. He is breathing inter reputedly. Is he going to be sick? He would ask for a sick leave from the office. Out of the window, a multilayered chaos is lined up with all of its menace. His boss will get upset saying again! He has no more patience left for the unsound personnel. His suspicion grew for that man. With the unironed pants and shirts, this miserable man's health sick excuses became boring. There is no work discipline in this man. In his office, he deliberated on the ways to fire this monument of laziness.

You are gnawing my soul. He didn't try to live without thinking. Without asking, free from concerns. Leave the house, the workplace is in an hour's distance. On the desks in the office, the documents piled up. The files are to run through. The guy is looking for an excuse to fire me. The files should be transferred to the computer. The file numbers of each file are attached.

All of the dilemmas of my soul are enumerated, and filed one by one.

His eyelids opened barely. Again it's a sunny day. For some time, there is no rain. He likes the cold, moreover the grayness in the sky. He feels like go be buried in darkness. Again, his inner voice is following him like a shadow. "You are gnawing me."

The Tomb of Sighs

This winter made many dead bodies. On one of our sides are the ruined cities, and the corpses of children and women are on the street. In my palm, "The Tree of Sighs". In the most eastern side of my heart, wrote Madak.

That place is frozen, quite forgetful. I snowed heavily. Istanbul is a white death. Everywhere is lit. The back streets and building sites of the city is dead white. We entered a new year. One of two lines should be written to the passing people. It is likely that we will not like the new year. "Several villages are under the water, the east of my heart…" Ah our tolerant states, and those of our soft and domicile expressions. Before the blackboard, the po-faced and armed officers lectured the dead. Dead bodies of the children, do not get scared; our elders and betters would know where you will be heading later, and what life you will wear as well as which dead you will play.

The east of my heart is waiting in between the legal and illegal orders. But we didn't like weapons at all, from where do come so many dead bodies. My eyes have been getting blind and fuzzy for days already. Hey doctor, I am now short-sighted. There is a smell of blood. This is not a delusion; the nightmares are the real deal. The street got silent, regardless of the language we translate into, the pain would be nothing but a lie. Again, Pollyanna, Madak crossed my mind. The lines are the most indirect confession about the date of our crime. Feelings are the only shelter we can hold on to. The city is buried under the snow. All of us stay at our houses sequestered. Our intimate stories intersected with our complicity in crime. The roads would always intersect though. All our intricate roads intersected from the east to the west, and from the west to the east at the same hell. "In short, they shot, we grew brother." Ah this is Ece Ayhan, what a great awareness we said as soon as we woke up, and the snow got lighter. Should we go out to the street? For several days, the street is not safe. There is a ban on living on the street. On the screens, roaring, upset and discontented faces. The authority wearing a tie is bossy, it's just time to join hands. Our soul is split up to the years, and every year we need to pick an offering to gods. Ah us, the ones deprived of imagination, if only we should be grateful for being able to breathe, we couldn't learn how to content ourselves with what we have. Ahs and Ohs wait at the bedside of geography. We were grown up with laments, and the houses of dead became our playground most of the time. The body got rotten, and the city smells bad. The snow while even hides the dead. If by change we get up from this nightmare, they would have us sleep again for having dreams. Laments and lullabies would be linked. By the way, my hand in on you.

I washed his dead body with poetry

You mister, would not know how to love a shadow

We got the creeps when we opened the window, shivered, and the cold penetrated into our body. We watched the shadows along the snow covered street. Following the indistinct night, only shadows remained, the souls would talk about the crime time. To make out what happened and what was happening, one need to have trans-eyes. This morning, our neighborhood made the Santa Claus see reason heroically, and every one of them is proud now. What's the point to hand out the body bag to the dead. This should not make the children happy, ours should not be spoiled. The entire city is ready for a ceremony which is deaf to streams, solemn, silent. Let us fire the mourners, the old Santa Clauses with their strong breathing carry the coffins. They will meet the young and fresh dead bodies through their most affectionate and fatherly attitudes. Like us, they too are the undertaker in our neighborhood. It's our job coming down from our ancestors to prepare the living ones for their last voyage. The powerful are shouting at the top of their voice. The snow will cover our date of crime. The city is stretching monotonously, with so many dying people, with multi-layered suffocation. The muezzin is reading the prayer for the dead again, how many of it within a day. The Grieving tunes are streaming on the screen.

One cannon ball hit one of the shanty houses. The woman was having her dinner on the ground, there is a curfew. The dead would not be included in the statistics, they are just a name section in the ID. The snow entered slowly into the room. There is a huge cavity on the ceiling. Life filled the gaps, if nothing else, the snow would cover the family scene having their dinner. Which painter painted this tragedy? Really, you are the dead of which village? The dead would choose carefully by their looks. This way, the decision would be make according to which one would deserve more of sorrow. A blizzard started now, and the snow is not tame anymore. There would be no snow painting out of this landscape. The snowmen have already been armed in our neighborhood. No part of our body is naked now, our souls are murky. The environment is not covered with the snow white, it is with the grayish white. Our desolateness is savage. We are cutting each other's throat in our wilds.

My memory would give birth every year to a fine, white foal

It was exhausted though

By running without stopping to remember

I felt chilly, would you please close the window. Television is too loud as well.

Peace demonstrations increased inside of me. My house demands silence. Please turn off the television.[4]

---

4 Poems from Didem Madak's poetry collection called *Ah'lar Ağacı / The Tree of Sighs.*

The Man at the Station

The road had fallen down on a faraway place. He rubbed his eyes, still sleepy from the last night. Mattery and weakened. He tried to figure out where did his looks go and lost.

– Yesterday you kept turning in the bed again.

As if he's not sleeping doesn't suffice, the woman complained about his not letting her sleep. This man has been sleeping half measure on the other corner of the bed for years. Supposedly it was a dream about travelling. If only he would have stayed at that hell he'd gone in his dream.

In his dream, at the train station he was carrying the suitcase he was holding tightly like a child being afraid of losing his toy. Last whistle. Perhaps there was no other station. There is no other town the train would be heading to. The station master was watching from afar the suspicious moves of this passenger. There are lights here and there in town. This town is also buried under mist for several days. After all, every year this mist menace would plague this region in every March for a couple of days. He glanced at the town situated around the buildings here and there...

– Again that town appeared in my dream. I have no idea about what station was that.

When he buried his head on the pillow and continued sleeping, he realized that he was talking to himself. When he got up slowly from the bed, he noticed the numbness in his body. He had embraced the weariness by traveler who traveled for hours. He went towards the window, and he gazed upon the dense light oozing between the sunshade. By taking the lid off, he watched the gray city. Apparently the mist had reached the city. He took out one cigarette from the box he had left on the coffee table in the night. The taste of the burning cigarette left a sour taste in his mouth. He has started to hate this damn thing a lot. It was 6. He had succeeded to get up that much early. He watched the woman on the other corner of the bed, who went to sleep grumblingly. He was startled by woman's order, turn off the light. He turned off the light of the room like an obeying child. His eye caught sight of his body appearing in the room. A hunchbacked and old body.

The last passenger of the last train to arrive to the station. The station master thought that birds of ill omen would come to this spooky station where nobody stops by. Even the lights in this houses here and there seemed obscure, artificial, and like a stage set put there recently to this sinister passenger. The man wanted to proceed leaving the station master's cold and suspicious looks behind. The master was like keeping a close watch on him. The stranger noticed the tea glass held by station master who moved away from the man. If only he would have a hot and strong tea. The station master had poured with pleasure tea in the glass from the teapot boiled on the stove, and watched the passenger leaving the station by slow steps. The shadow of the station master was being reflected on the wall already through the burning in the stove. There was nowhere to go. He noticed that the steps of the man got slower, and the passenger shivered down his spine. He moved forward inside the mist.

He gazed off into the view of the city's crowded and side-to-side life out of the window. He startled. In the morning the house gets cold. His hand touched his beard. It was time to cut it. The new resident of the city tried to find the gray sky in between a couple of skyscrapers. It was tiring for him to look inside the mist. He was contented with looking at the wetness on the housetops by the night's rain. He thought that the building got paler inside the mist.

– What are you doing here Mister?

This single question asked by the station master to the stranger was etched on his memory. He had avoided the man through short replies. As the station master, who didn't want to insist, was moving away from his side, he kind of thought that it is not a good idea to mess with this type of men. The stove was reactivated with some sawdust thrown to the coal stove in the Station Master's room. He dreamt of the spreading heat reached his face turned to red out of cold and his hands which were about to freeze. He got rid of the feeling of cold for a moment. He noticed a couple of shrubs gathered on the high elevations of the town here and there in the mist. As he was proceeding silently, the fear inside of him grew.

– Why on earth you are going to set the alarm, if you are going to get up early, man alive!

He flinched by the alarm of the watch. The same rage on the face of the woman. He got it better that it was one of the compulsory residents of the house when he heard the sound. He wanted to move away from the room, he had to shave and get dressed. The light of the bathroom was left on in the night. His beard got quite rough. As he was spreading the foam on his face, he thought about his dislike of shaving.

The station got lost inside the mist. He took his steps in desolateness of a cemetery. If you can't see hand in front of face, then becoming blind doesn't cause a harm. He dropped himself in the infinite gap. And he felt that his shadow took the shape of giant.

The Common Fly, The School Bell, etc.

For days he has been dragging my heels to go to school. The watchman teased him, you are the night guy I think, he said. His close and grinning state offended him.

When you exit the school after the day starts getting dark, then there would be no power left in you. His eyes caught sight of the dirty, ugly blue color of the school walls. His course is for the twelve grade. For some time, all of them became a test monster. They did not finish the same test book within two semesters, this was another issue. As soon as the teachers bell was rung, he was in the class room again. It was his usual punctuality. The second he entered the classroom, he faced with the bloodshot eyes of Murat out of sleeplessness. The ginger cat had taken refuge in the classroom, constantly touring the room from one lap to another. Now purring on the top of the desk. Afterwards, in a second it just stood up and settled on Murat's lap. Last year this boy happened to be the arch enemy of the discipline regulations. He was walking in the class room like a ghost. I became such a sinister, bad-tempered guy because of these boys. Look the eyes, for sure they are cursing at me inwardly.

The brunette girl in front is reading the text in the book. She is crazy about getting high marks; this is the reason for her flattery. She raises her hand to talk through hat. What is the writer wants to tell about, children? What kind of man is the protagonist of the novel in your opinion? They didn't get bored of having us introduce the same text for years. Some commonplace explanation should be given to the class. Maybe there would be some students taking notes so that they would answer the questions in the exam.

Nobody is in the mood of listening to him. He writes the names of several novels, their expression techniques, lots of other things be them necessary or not, on the black boar in such a size that they can be read easily.

- Consciousness stream, flashback was asked at the Higher Education Competence Exam, children. Writer would map of the human soul in this type of works. *Really, if they map my soul, what would happen? Sometimes though, the so-called inner voice is the confession of being lunatic.*

Such a great expression, he thinks. Again, Murat's eye is at the wall clock. Most probably he thinks that after being saved from failing his class because of his absence from school upon thousands of requests, now he has no other option to cower and doze off. The common fly not getting bored of walking inside the classroom lads near me for a couple of times. For as long as I've known, I don't like this fly tribe. Following the fly menace's attack, a sweet itching comes in.

The roar in the classroom doesn't stop. The hall monitor is walking along the corridor holding a notebook. Class president Ali shows up at that very moment.

-Absentees?

- The same persons, my teacher.

- Murat did not sleep enough, I think. You must certainly had memorized the test books last night. Your mother had not come to the parent-teacher meeting. At the end of the education year, she would be glued to me. These thoughts are passing through my mind. Sit in your seat now, my daughter. *This girl is in a rush to send a message to her lover. The boy must have sent to you such nice words since you have that grinning expression on your face.*

His voice sounds cynical. While burying his head into his coat, Murat is disdaining to give an answer. He is always pissed off with this boy. He was the one who at tempted to racketeer from the ninth graders. It's the business as usual even though he warned him so many times. His acting this way always makes him extremely upset. They are fond of this boy. Apparently all girls of the class are falling for him for his being handsome, heavy set boy. At that moment, Murat is looking at him as if he was caught red-handed. After some students left for basic high schools, the classroom size dropped down almost to twenty.

He intends to go about the mind of the class. As if all of them speak of the same thing. *We don't like school, teacher. We are not much of fond of you either.* Each of them is of such breed that if it were an affectionate teacher to deal with them, then they would step all over that teacher. *Ok, let us free you soon from eight hours long of imprisonment.* At that moment, the hall monitor calls on Murat. Murat hastily gets up. You can tell looking at his face that he is on thorns. There is no trace of his comfort a moment ago. *There should be a reason for his being called every so often.* While all of these were passing through his mind, the common fly land on the teacher's desk unquietly.

When looked at the wall watch, he realizes that the last class was not really over. The roar in the class is cut for a moment. Without several minutes passed, Murat enters the classroom, without feeling the need to say anything. His face looks deadly pale. Seemingly Teacher Mehmet scolded him. *Murat, let us try with you the consciousness stream, ha! Maybe in your home, they must have raised a hell of a row. On top of that, your father must have made a verbal attack. We had to put up with you for four years type of words must have flown in the air. You became a big name, when the high school is over, you would be on your own, kind of saying his final word.*

He was sorry to say a word when he sat in his desk. On every occasion he looked at that boy, he thought he was face to face with a wall. Why doesn't he call on him to get near him? He forwent his decision. He was the one who spilled out hatred against their classroom teacher Mrs. Melahat just one week ago. Even he enraged their matron like woman.

Ayşe and Beren are asking about one or two questions in the test book they had difficulty to answer

-You should go through pronouns in my opinion. Here they were used in the place of adjective.

His nerves are shot. Murat's looks are lost in the void. Evidently, when you hold no brief for someone, then his or her every action would offend the eye. Teacher Mehmet appears by the door's threshold out of nowhere.

This man would not show off in the middle of the class so easily. He gets confused by this situation.

-Well dear teacher, this child's mother has been in the hospital for years. The family hid it in order the teacher would not know about this issue. There is not much hope as you can imagine. I would recommend that It would be alright if you don't push him too much. I had words with him lately, yet afterwards I felt sorry.

As if sensing that the talk was about him, Murat was watching carefully two teachers by standing on the door threshold.

- You see, the reason for the eyes being bloodshot is now known. Why don't these children tell us their problems at all?

- Even we didn't have any news about it, I swear. The father is a trash, he left them years ago.

His distress was growing while he was listening to the deputy principal on the door threshold. When he returned to the classroom, the entire class was watching him with alarm. Obviously, they thought that Murat had a problem with the school. You consoled yourself for years for being such a good teacher. He got upset with himself inwardly. His eye caught sight of the crack on the wall. As is it has been growing every day. Every corner of the school was already in full of holes. *Where did the pang of guilt come from? Ultimately you are not responsible for the illness of the woman. It's so difficult to understand a human being. Those thoughts were exhausting him increasingly.*

There are five minutes to go before the bell rings. A few of them will gather by the door. As if there is an award for the first exiting. Ayşe touches on Murat's shoulder rigorously. At that moment he opens his eyes with a heavy heart. At the time close to the bell, he draws a circle on the empty paper at the table. Then he painted black inside that circle resentfully. *Still the hall monitor didn't take the class notebook.* For a moment, they came eye to eye with Murat. *Well teacher, I would be not touring in school crying and saying that my mother is going to die.* They both averted their gaze. The gaze of the boy got lost in void involuntarily. Murat, you are to leave the school notebook at the administration. *Well bonehead, is that you had a good communication with the child in the end? You are a seasoned teacher so to speak.* At that moment, the lazy fly goes away flying out of the open window.

When he moved away from the school gate, he started smoking the only cigarette left in the box. *Till tomorrow, you should get away from the furrier's shop. Again, a bad cough. You should quit this damn thing.* Several people are walking away after saying good evening dear teacher. Murat being collapsed on the bank at the park on the corner, trying not to be seen anyone. You see, he cowards at a corner *Should I sit by him. A teacher should keep a distance with students. You knew it this way for years. I too started smoking this damn thing in high school. Do you think this boy would mock me by saying it has nothing to do with you being student in that old time? This boy may run hot and cold.* His thoughts are disappearing in the smoke of the cigarette. He may as well catch a dolmush at this hour. A roar rising from behind. The voices get mixed among the crowd of the students. If his mother dies, his father would not let Murat come to school. The man is nearly about to divorce the woman. Murat's mind is as quiet as a mouse, and a common fly is landing on the head of the boy in the distant corner of the park at that very moment.

The Whisperer

The town having woken up with the echo of the morning call to prayer, is crashing under the weight of the old secret despite the day seems to be a new one. The silently spreading the smell of coffee among streets, is whispering the hidden realities inside the cup in Zeliha's palm. While the old spaewife was rotating the cup with her trembling hands, sees a shadow rooted in the coffee grounds; the trace of the small girl is not erased, being frozen at the bottom of the cup.

"She didn't go," Zeliha murmurs. "She was always her, always here; in our shadows, in our whisper…"

The traces of the coffee grounds extend like a small, thin hand; as if that help demanding hand is squeezing the soul of the town. But nobody seems to hear, nobody seems to see. As the town keeps quiet, the shadow of the girl in the deepens. Closing the cup, Zeliha bows her head, knowing that the traces of these coffee grounds are the silent scream of the mute town, and she keeps it like a secret.

Even though the town would close their eyes, that shadow, comes alive every morning again in Zeliha's cup, like a curse.